Whispers Never Spoken

Molly O'Connor

TotalRecall Publications, Inc.
1103 Middlecreek
Friendswood, Texas 77546
281-992-3131 281-482-5390 Fax
www.totalrecallpress.com

All rights reserved. Except as permitted under the United States Copyright Act of 1976, No part of this publication may be reproduced, stored in a retrieval system, or transmitted in any form or by any means electronic or mechanical or by photocopying, recording, or otherwise without prior permission of the publisher. Exclusive worldwide content publication / distribution by TotalRecall Publications, Inc.

Copyright © 2021 by Molly O'Connor
Background Cover Graphic: Shutterstock

ISBN: 978-1-64883-111-9
UPC: 6 43977 4110-6

FIRST EDITION
1 2 3 4 5 6 7 8 9 10

The scanning, uploading and distribution of this book via the Internet or via any other means without the permission of the publisher is illegal and punishable by law. Please purchase only authorized electronic editions, and do not participate in or encourage electronic piracy of copyrighted materials. Your support of the author's rights is appreciated.

To my children and grandchildren, my many friends near and far, you bring me joy each and every day.

Chapter 1

Stark white against the black quartz counter, the envelope threatened, demanding her attention. There was no visible return address and the postmark was blurred. She couldn't see where it originated and did not recognize the handwriting. It lay there glaring the whole time she made and ate her breakfast of cereal and an omelet loaded with veggies and cheese. She downed three cups of coffee with cream, no sugar. No matter what she was doing, she never took her eyes off the envelope, not when she reached across for the sugar to sweeten her cereal, being careful not to tip over the bowl, and not when she set her bowl of Shredded Wheat beside her spoon. She chewed slowly as she contemplated what might be in the letter. She moved it when she wiped the counter. She stood over it, drumming her fingertips on the countertop. Why was she procrastinating? Why was she so hesitant to open it?

Ann reached deep into her memory to see if she could remember ever having seen that handwriting before. The cursive was small, cramped and angled slightly upward. When she pulled the mail out of the postal box, number 15, third row right side, she had not noticed anything different — just the usual bills, letters and notices. Then when she got home, she sorted it according to what category each belonged. This was a daily morning routine: one pile for Ray, her husband, mostly bills and computer stuff, her fan letters (she was a fiction author) and personal stuff. Most of her letters were addressed to her pen name, Alice Turnbell. This one was addressed to herself, Ann Rogers,

2345 Sweet Apple Drive, Kanata. There was no reason to suspect that the contents were not something she wanted to read but yet she dreaded opening it, fearing what it might say.

"This is ridiculous! Open the damn thing!"

Her voice echoed in the empty kitchen. She took her coffee to the double sink and leaned her firm butt against the counter as she sipped the last mouthful of her coffee, then turned and rinsed the mug. She always used the same mug, with Running Gal written across numerous pairs of colourful running shoes. She caught a glimpse of her reflection in the patio window. Dressed in old, faded Wranglers that had been washed to soft and an equally over-washed sweatshirt, she was ready to hit the trail. This was her running outfit, which she wore most mornings as she ran at a steady pace for seven to ten kilometres. Today, her shoulder-length brown hair was tied back into a neat ponytail but a few straggler strands always escaped and curled along her nape. Her one vanity was her slender figure: at 5'6" she carried no extra weight.

"Okay then. Here we go." Ann opened the dishwasher and stacked her rinsed dishes and coffee mug on the rack, pushed the sleeves of her faded blue sweatshirt up her arm and reached for the letter. Sliding the wood block knife stand from the back of the counter closer to her, she selected a small one and slit the thin envelope. It contained a single sheet of tri-folded paper. She smoothed the page flat and read:

Dear Ann
I might be your biological father. Please call me 743 555-4412.
Bert

Well that was a hoot — obviously the wrong Ann. She let out a long, slow breath that she hadn't even realized she'd been holding. She was about to rip it up when something made her think again. Always curious and often accused of being nosy, she read the phone number again. Her laptop was on the table so she slipped around the counter and moved to the nearest chair, straightened the keyboard and entered the ten-digit number. It came up "number private". She then checked the area code to see where it was located and learned that it was in California. This explained nothing since people took their cell numbers with them even when they changed location, but it might be where this letter came from — however, a number originating in one state could be anywhere in the country. The only person she knew in California was an elderly aunt on her father's side. Was this a prank? It did not make any sense. Besides, her mother and father were high-school sweethearts married right out of college. Whatever the note meant, and who it was intended for, she did not have a clue.

Her cell slithered across the desk as it vibrated, indicating an incoming call. Ann stood up and reached across the desk to capture the escaping phone and looked at the caller ID, to see it was her mother. She stabbed Answer …

"Hey, Mom. How are you this morning?"

"Well dear, as usual, the news reports aren't good, the weather sucks and I have to go out for a dental session. I do have an appointment to get my hair done though — that should cheer me up. Other than that, everything is peachy. How about you?"

"I'm moving a bit slow after Jason and I hiked twenty kilometres through the Gatineau hills yesterday. Lordy, I found muscles I forgot I had." Ann was stretching one leg after the other as she talked. "I'm getting ready to go for a run in a few minutes. I need to loosen up."

"I can never understand why you run. Your friend Jason and you always overdo it. Certainly was not something I ever did. As you know, I did a little gymnastics in high school and was a cheerleader and that's about it. Yoga's more my speed. I sometimes wonder how Ray feels about you running with another man."

"For God's sake, Mom, Jason's as light as can be and he's married to Warren. I know you don't get it, Mom, but I need to wake up the endorphins and breathe fresh morning air. After a good run, my creative juices flow, I come alive. If it is a sunny day, all the better."

"Well, dear. You enjoy your run and I'll suffer through the dentist."

"Oh, quick question. Does the name Bert mean anything to you?" Ann was walking to the kitchen as she talked.

Ann wasn't sure but she thought she heard her mother pause and take a quick breath intake before she replied.

"No. Why, dear?"

The tone in Elsie's voice was low, hesitant and her answer was slightly strained.

Ann waited a moment before she answered. "It's nothing. I'm considering using it for one of my characters in the new book. As you know, I like to get feedback on what I'm writing."

"Funny. You've never asked me for my opinion before. But you write whatever you feel works for your audience. You have a strong following. They'll love whatever you do."

"Well I haven't made the best-seller list yet, but maybe some day."

"Since you asked my opinion, another name might be better. That one doesn't do anything for me. Anyway, I'm off."

The call disconnected.

Ann glanced at the phone then the letter. There was something in the way her mother skirted around the question that alerted Ann's suspicion. *She's lying.* Ann folded the page, stuffed it back into the envelope and shoved it into the back pocket of her jeans.

"Who was that? Elsie? Everything all right? You seem distracted."

Ray strode across the kitchen, around the black countertop and leaned down to give Ann a peck on the cheek. He reached up into the glass-fronted cupboard for a mug, and then poured a cup of coffee. He added three spoons of sugar and a generous helping of cream.

"Fine. She's fine. She's off to the dentist no doubt to have her teeth whitened then the hairdresser for her monthly colour job. She has to keep up the Barbie Doll appearance. Oh, that wasn't kind. I'm off to hit the trail. I'd better do a quick bathroom stop after three cups of coffee."

"Did you look after Jade?"

"I fed her yesterday."

It was a family joke that Jade was Ann and Ray's only child, yet hard to explain to others how a jade tree became so personal. It had been a small plant given to Ann and Ray as a housewarming gift shortly after they were married. It had come with a short manual of how to care for it. Ann had read the manual out loud at the party. Everyone contributed ridiculous additional care-giving ideas that had caused a lot of laughter. When the raucous mood settled down, Ray announced that it was going to be a lot of work — almost as much as caring for a child — so the little plant had to have an official name. After a group consensus, it was deemed that it was female and Jade was to be her name. That was seventeen years ago and Jade had grown and flourished. Every December, she blossomed with an abundance of delicate white flowers that clung to the plant long after the blooms had withered. It was not unusual to still have dried flowers on the tree in July. Jade had been transplanted several times and was now a tree that stood about five feet tall. The leaves were thick and glossy, a picture of health.

Ray was laughing. "Have a good run. I'm meeting the boys for breakfast at Timmy's. I'll see you later." Ray, dressed in jeans and a white cable-stitched sweater, reached for his denim jacket as he headed out the back entrance through the garage.

Ann wrapped a scarf around her neck and put on a fleece vest then left the house by the front door. The skies were cloudy but the cool temperatures were perfect for running. There had not been any snow for days so the trail would be clear. She turned left and headed for Abbott Street and the Trans Canada Trail.

Chapter 2

Elsie stared at her cell phone and quickly dropped it into her purse as if it were on fire. She took off her reading glasses and put them on the dresser top. She took a last-minute glance in the mirror, tucked a stray bit of hair behind her ear and, gathering up her purse, left the bedroom. As she headed along the back hallway to the garage, she stopped and slumped against the doorjamb. Her car keys jiggling in her hand, she was shaking.

Why after all these years is this having such an affect on me? It was simply a coincidence. Get on with your day and don't give it another thought.

Before she opened the door, she called back toward the den, "Stan, I'm off to the dentist. Please make sure you put out the garbage and sweep the garage."

Once in her baby-blue Toyota Prius, Elsie used the remote to open the garage door, touched the starter, adjusted the volume of her pre-selected radio station and slowly backed out. She pointed the remote at the door and closed it. Driving slowly along Riverside Drive to Heron Road, her thoughts drifted back to her high school days — back to 1963. She could almost hear the giggling bouncing off the walls of the gymnasium.

The cheerleader squad was a close-knit bunch of fifteen mostly 16-year-olds. This was the intermediate group, the next level up from the junior team. As a cheerleader, Elsie learned intricate steps to lively music and some simple gymnast elements. Coach was talented at making the slightly uncoordinated group seem synchronized by giving them simple routines. Elsie remembered clearly the day they were issued batons — these were to be twirled and thrown during to their routines. Coach thought it would demonstrate an element of skill not shown before and that it would be a crowd pleaser. She called for everyone's attention and deftly held one of the slim sticks in her right hand. She was dressed in a short, pleated, green-plaid skort that she used to wear golfing. It looked like a skirt but was really shorts with a skirt; with it, she wore a yellow T-shirt.

"Baton twirling requires skillful coordination and extraordinary control of the human body. It requires a certain amount of flexibility in order to properly execute baton, dance, and do gymnastics elements. You'll be given special dance movements designed for baton twirling which will promote expression of the body. These will show off your strength, flexibility and physical fitness. The beauty of movement and harmony is important to demonstrate the body's coordination with the manipulation of the baton. Now listen carefully. The foundation of baton twirling is the thumb toss. This trick is accomplished from the middle of the baton. Please note that the stick part is called the shaft. What is the stick part called?"

"The shaft," the girls shouted in unison.

"One end has a large ball and the other a smaller one. The baton is held in one hand at your waist before raising it for performance. The baton is then rolled over the thumb and a slight hand movement lifts it into the air. The thumb toss can be increased in difficulty with one or more spins done under the toss, cartwheels, front walkovers, illusions or many more tricks. What is the basis of baton twirling?"

"The thumb toss."

"The baton can be tossed from either hand, but proficiency in both hands is preferable. The baton can be caught blind behind the head, at the side, under a kick, under one or both legs or in front. Other tosses include the open hand toss and flat spin toss. Watch as I demonstrate."

The team watched, amazed at how Coach flipped the wand and threw it into the air, twirled around and caught it as it came down. Elsie started to clap, followed by the entire team.

"What I just showed you is pretty basic. It looks easy when I do it, but you will find it does require practice to become skilled and confident. Practice and more practice will be needed until the moves become second nature. Now each of you come and pick out a baton and we will start."

The girls scrambled to the table set against the wall and each took a baton and returned to their delegated spot to await instruction.

"Watch me roll the stick over my thumb." Coach deftly turned the baton over and held it upright. "Now you try."

The gymnasium echoed one bang after another as the batons dropped from the cheerleaders' hands onto the polished hardwood flooring.

"Okay then. Pick them up and try again."

After a few tries, most of the girls were able to do this one small manoeuvre except for Elsie. As she bent over to collect the fallen baton yet again, she looked up to see Stan Rider watching her. Her cheeks flushed red.

Oh my God! This is so embarrassing. I am the clumsiest girl in the whole squad. And this is supposed to be the easiest step. How am I ever going to ever be able to throw it in the air without making a fool of myself? Stan must think I'm such an idiot.

Retrieving her baton, she returned it to the table and raced for the change rooms.

"Hey Elsie. What's the hurry?"

"Lordy, I am so spastic. I'll never manage to hold on to the damn thing let alone throw it up and catch it."

Barbara knew that Elsie had a huge crush on Stan and if she sympathized, Elsie would burst into tears. Barbara shook her heavy head of wavy brunette hair.

"Well, you always like to play the comedian. That little display was really funny. Portraying a drunk trying to hold a baton. Clever." Barbara winked and Elsie smiled in relief then started laughing.

"You always have a way of making me feel better." Elsie started staggering about like she was drunk.

Both girls doubled over laughing and were still giggling when they left the change rooms. When they stepped out into the October sunshine, Stan was leaning against the school sign, blocking some of the letters of South High School so it read South Hi hool.

Barbara winked at Elsie as they prepared to walk past. Elsie turned her face away so she avoided having to face Stan.

Barbara and Elsie walked along Campeau Street and parted at the golf course. Barbara lived in one of the large two-storey houses backing onto the golf course. Elsie continued farther to Kanata Street where she lived in a more mid-income area. As she approached the driveway of her red-brick-sided bungalow, her mother was just pulling in.

"Give me a hand, Elsie. I have bags and bags of groceries."

Elsie adjusted her backpack and grabbed four bags.

"Honey, you look like you just lost your best friend. What's the matter?" Elsie's mother set a load of groceries on the kitchen counter and watched her daughter. Elsie's long, straight, ash-blonde hair shone in the afternoon light pouring in through the kitchen window. But she did not shine. In fact, she was quite sullen.

"I'm just such a klutz. Coach introduced batons to us and I couldn't even toss it once. I am so uncoordinated. I suck at everything."

"Really? Well maybe we can solve that. Help me put this stuff away then meet me in the den. I have a little surprise for you."

Once the groceries were stashed in their designated places, Elsie grabbed an apple and her backpack. She changed out of her deep-navy short skirt, white blouse and navy knee socks (her school uniform), and into old jeans and a grey sweatshirt. She was munching away when she rounded the hallway to the den. To her amazement, she saw her mother throwing a baton high in the air, spin around and catch it.

"What! You know how to twirl the baton?"

"Sweetheart, I guess I neglected to tell you that I was provincial champion for many years. I am the twirling queen." With that she tossed the baton turned and caught it at her back, tossed it again, turned and brought it through her legs, threw it high in the air and caught it neatly. "Wasn't sure I could still do this stuff."

"Mom, you're amazing!"

"And you will be, too. I think your biggest problem will be to overcome the fact that you are left-handed. Not easy in this game. Both hands have to be equal. Now, I want you to try it with your left hand first. Once you can do the thumb rollover with that hand, you will know how it feels and can then transfer what you learned to the right hand. For you, it's twice as hard to start, but you'll have the advantage when the rest of the team has to switch and use their left hand. Mind you, most of the manoeuvres are done right-handed so you, my dear, do face a challenge."

Elsie threw the apple core into the trash bin before she reached for the baton her mother held out to her. She listened closely as she was instructed on how to roll it over very slowly.

"Good. Now increase the speed a wee bit."

Elsie sent the baton flying across the tiles.

"No, no. When I say a wee bit, I mean a wee bit. Try it again slowly. Good. Now increase the speed a very little bit. That's it. Keep trying those movements over and over, increasing the speed ever so slightly when you feel confident enough. Have fun. I have to change out of this go-out-in-public outfit and put on my black sweats. Then I'm going to get supper ready."

Elsie did as her mother instructed, dropping the baton a few times but within an hour she had increased the speed by twice.

"Mom, Mom! Come see. I've got it. Come watch me." The smile on her face told the story of her success.

Bit by bit, Elsie worked with her mother until she could do a simple toss with both hands. Elsie walked away, tossing and catching, tossing and catching, over and over again. The following day, she practised with her right hand. Her mother was right. She was able to transfer the ability she learned from working with her left hand to her right. She could hardly wait for cheerleading practice.

The cheerleaders met twice a week and Elsie felt confident as she strode across the gymnasium and picked up a baton. Coach repeated the lesson from the other day and Elsie had no problem following the instruction.

Thanks, Mom.

As the group moved to the next steps, Elsie was smiling away as she hadn't dropped her baton once; and when Coach told the girls to try the same thing with the other hand, Elsie did a quick flip and a simple toss.

"Elsie. Very good. Have you been practising?'

"Yes, Coach. My mother helped."

"Well, girls, each of you can take a baton home to practise. Mind you, you are responsible for not losing it and returning it in good shape. Please sign the Take-out sheet so I know who has batons."

Elsie did not take one.

"Well, you sure overcame your dropitis."

"Barb, I'm one lucky gal. My mother was the baton-twirling champion when she was younger. She's amazing! She can do almost anything with her baton. She's also a great teacher."

Both girls changed out of their blue gym bloomers and into their uniforms before grabbing their backpacks and heading for the school exit. It was a bleak day with grey skies and threats of rain. They hurried along, anxious to get home before they got soaked.

"Hey, Else. Got a minute?" Stan was, once again, leaning against the school sign.

The girls stopped and Elsie stepped to the side so she was facing Stan.

Lowering his voice so Barbara wouldn't hear, Stan asked Elsie if she would like to go to a movie Saturday evening.

Elsie felt heat rising to her face and knew she was blushing. "Yea, sure. That would be great."

Stan pushed away from the sign and fell into step with the girls. This was to be their first date and within weeks they were going steady. And steady they stayed all through high school, and when Stan went to Carleton University, and Elsie to Algonquin College. Stan immediately was hired by Bell Canada in the finance department and Elsie landed a position at Canada Post in Human Resources. They planned an autumn wedding with a one-week honeymoon in Quebec City. Within two years, they had bought a bungalow in Alta Vista and to this day still lived there.

They had been married five years before Elsie became pregnant and they became parents to a beautiful baby girl. Ann was truly a blessing as Elsie never conceived again.

Chapter 3

Ann had double-tied her sneaker laces before she hurried outside. The house was a block from Abbott Street and Shea Road, very close to the Trans Canada Trail. Once she crossed Abbott, she picked up her stride and the distance fell behind her as she raced along the pavement, heading west. The path was lined with trees showing a haze of soft, green, new leaves, and the grass was showing signs of growing, foreshadowing warmer days to come. Strained muscles in her legs eased as she got up to speed, and within minutes, she was at the intersection of Village Square Park and Main Street. The light was red and there was light traffic. She stopped to wait for the light to change and bent over to relax her neck and to stretch her upper leg muscles. Her thoughts ran through the storyline of her latest novel. She often overcame writing blocks as she ran and mulled over the plots. She had left her protagonist alone on a train, devastated at her romance falling apart. A horrendous noise shattered her thoughts, and her immediate reaction was to duck to the left. A small projectile flew past her, narrowly missing her head.

What the —?

Straightening up, Ann looked toward Main Street and saw that a large box truck had slammed into a compact car, crushed the driver's side, and pushed it toward the curb. Ann heard screaming mixed with the grating noise of metal on metal. She watched in horror as the vehicles slid sideways and the car was pushed hard against the curb near where she was standing. It tilted onto its side.

Ann, having stepped back several feet, had narrowly missed

being hit. She could smell scorched metal and watched fuel puddle onto the sidewalk. She saw two small children trapped in the back seat and, who she surmised was their mother, in the driver's seat.

She ran around to the roadside and without thinking, she carefully set her right foot on the undercarriage, tested it to make sure it was solid and used it to climb onto the back fender. Then she pulled herself along by the door handle. Leaning forward, she reached for the front door handle and pulled with all her might. It wouldn't move, the frame was bent and she couldn't budge it. She eased along the edge to the back fender and balanced by bracing herself with one foot on the tire and one on the fender. With forced strength, she was able to yank the door open. She made sure it held in place so it would not slam shut on her as she eased herself into the cavity.

A small girl about five years old watched her with large brown eyes. Her nose was running from crying and she was trembling.

"Hi, sweety. My name is Ann and I'm going to undo your seatbelt and get you out of here. Don't be afraid. You're going to be fine. Are you hurt?" Ann looked into large staring eyes that watched her like a frightened deer. The little head shook from side to side.

Keeping her voice soft and reassuring, Ann kept talking non-stop to keep the child calm. "What's your name? I'm going to undo your seatbelt and help you get out of the car."

"Tammy." Ann barely heard the stammered reply.

"Is that your pet bunny, Tammy?" Ann saw that Tammy was clutching a squished, pink, stuffed rabbit firmly against her waist. "We'll have to save him, too. Hold on to him real tight."

She made sure the stuffed toy was secure, undid the seatbelt and grabbed the front of Tammy's red snowsuit and pulled her to her chest. She glanced sideways and noticed a young man was leaning into the opening. Turning with care, making sure Tammy was not frightened, she kept smiling into Tammy's face as she prepared to hand her off to his waiting arms.

"I am going to hand Tammy out to you then get her brother." She turned to Tammy. "Okay, kiddo? Ready? Okay, sweetheart. Here goes."

With a strong, careful lift, she reached and shoved Tammy toward the waiting arms and felt her being carried away. The smell of gasoline was burning the back of Ann's throat. She rubbed her nose against her sleeve to get some relief then leaned over the front seat to see how the mother was faring. She was pretty sure she wasn't conscious but spoke to her anyway.

"You okay? Can you move?" The mother was not moving. "Can you move anything? I got Tammy out safely and am about to undo the baby. What's his name? Your children will need you. They're very frightened. Try to slide over to the passenger side away from the steering wheel." There was no answer but Ann saw her stir and heard a soft moan.

Ann undid the baby who was rigid with fear, and whimpering. "Hey, champ. When you get outside, you're going to see a big fire engine coming. Listen. Can you hear it?" Ann could hear the sirens.

The baby leaned into Ann's waiting arms and held on tight around her neck.

By bracing herself against the front seat, Ann was able to hand him off to the young man who, once again, waited to receive him. She heard a voice. The mother's. Ann let out a big sigh of relief.

It soon became evident that the mother could not get her seatbelt released and couldn't move her legs.

"Get out of there! The car's on fire!"

Ann ignored the caution yelled by someone outside.

"Are you okay?" she yelled to the mother. "Stay calm. The firemen have just arrived. They'll likely have to cut the door away. Your children are safe. You're going to be all right." She kept uttering comforting words to the woman who was now crying hysterically.

A fireman leaned in to where Ann was and spoke to her. "Ma'am, please take my hand. I'm going to haul you out of there. The front door is jammed so we're going to have to break in through the front window to get the driver out. You need to leave now."

The heat was getting unbearable but Ann, leaning over into the front, tried to get the mother's seatbelt to release. Flames were licking the side of the front when the buckle finally let go and Ann grabbed the mother under her armpits and pushed her forward toward the passenger side and the front window. She heard the window drop away and saw another pair of arms reach toward the woman and pull her free. Another arm reached through the back door and grabbed the waist of Ann's jeans to help her out.

"Careful. There's some jagged metal right beside you," the voice yelled.

Ann heard her jeans rip before she saw the piece of jagged steel on her right. She pulled free and maneuvered around the sharp metal as she reached for an outstretched hand. They had barely made it to the sidewalk before the car was totally ablaze. The mother was being whisked away on a stretcher and Ann gave a weak smile to her helper. He assisted her to the curb to a safe spot and let her fall to the grass.

"Is the mom okay? When I pulled her free, she screamed in pain."

"She's being carried over to the park benches where her children are. All I know is she's bleeding and paramedics are working on her. The children are wrapped in blankets and are on the bench beside her. What a mess. Are you all right? That was one brave thing you did. Are you hurt? You're bleeding."

Ann got slowly to her feet and bending over rested her hands on her knees to ease her light-headedness. She felt her legs quiver and she was unsteady. She saw blood oozing through her jeans at her calf and felt it running down her leg to her ankle.

She felt arms slide around her waist. "Easy now. You're experiencing shock. You'll need to sit for a while." A short, stocky medic was supporting Ann and directing her over to a vacant bench. "It's not uncommon to experience a delayed reaction. That was quick thinking on your part. You are the hero of the day. I expect the police will want to speak with you."

Ann leaned into the female medic and let herself be guided to a vacant bench some distance from the mother and children. She was shaking uncontrollably and tears were streaming down her cheeks.

"For God's sake, why am I crying? I'm not hurt."

"That's shock. Happens when the blood pressure elevates then drops rapidly."

A warm blanket was draped over her back. "Take deep breaths and concentrate on relaxing your hands, then your arms, then your shoulders until you stop shaking."

The medic's soft voice calmed Ann and she was able to look

up and take in the scene around her. Three police cars had arrived along with a fire engine and two ambulances. Hoses were thoroughly dousing the car leaning against the right curb and the truck that was stalled across the left lane. A police officer was directing traffic around the vehicles. The truck driver was being interviewed by two officers on the other side of the street. He was holding what looked like a wallet. She thought there were five police officers and six medics, but the scene kept shifting so she wasn't sure.

Ann felt her breathing evening out and other than feeling really wobbly, she was much improved. The medic had rolled up her pant leg and was wiping away the blood so she could see how badly Ann was injured.

"I'll have you patched up in no time. It's only a surface wound and will not require stitches. Do you feel dizzy at all?"

"A wee bit." Ann saw a tall, older police officer approaching her. The sidewalk was crowded with curious bystanders. Ann noted that there were two women with babies in strollers and an older couple. A teen wearing a helmet was standing beside her bike.

"Ma'am? I'm Officer Whalen. I have a few questions. You're today's hero. May I sit beside you?"

Whalen sat down when Ann nodded. His bulk made the bench shake and Ann watched this uniformed man, probably in his late fifties, with short-cropped, grey hair. He reminded her of the Friendly Giant. "Were you driving, ma'am?"

"No. I was running along the Trail. I had stopped for the traffic light to change to green."

"Can you tell me what you witnessed? Take your time."

"I heard it before I saw it. I was bending over stretching my calves and getting ready to set off again. When I looked up, I saw that black truck pushing against the car. It was angled so that its front bumper was pushing against the sedan's driver's door," Ann pointed toward the old rusted truck. "It happened so fast. Then the car hit the curb and upended. I heard screaming and saw children in the back seat so, without thinking, I climbed on the car and pulled the back door open, and jumped in to help the children escape. That's how I got in."

"Your action likely saved those children's lives, not to mention the mother's. That young man over there took the children from you and handed them safely off to a female officer." He was pointing at a tall lean youth that was standing in awkward silence with his long arms dangling at his sides. Another policeman approached him, put his arms around the teen's shoulders and led him to another bench. "That young man reacted quickly, too." He will be queried by that other officer so we'll have his statement on record, too."

The teen's curly brown hair was sweaty and plastered to his forehead. He looked intense and embarrassed as he explained what he knew. He kept rubbing his hands down the side of baggy grey sweats.

"Oh, I need to thank him." Ann tried to stand up.

"No, not right now. You need to stop shaking and crying."

Ann wiped her eyes and reached into her pocket for a tissue to wipe her runny nose but had none. She looked down and saw that her trembling hands were scraped and also bleeding. The medic smiled, handed Ann a tissue and with practised efficiency, soon had Ann's hands swabbed clean and was busy applying ointment.

Ann saw the mother on a gurney, wrapped in a white blanket, being wheeled toward one of the two ambulances. A navy-blue car skidded to a stop and a man in a business suit leapt out and ran over to the woman. She immediately reached up into his arms.

Ann assumed he was the husband and father.

The mother tried to get up holding tightly to her husband.

Ann heard the medic tell her to lie back, that she needed to be taken to the hospital. She saw her urge her husband and point over to Ann. He picked up the baby and took his daughter's hand as she clung to his leg. Ann stood to meet him.

There was no need for words. They simply wrapped themselves around each other. The father thanked Ann over and over again. The children stared up at her not fully understanding why their father was hugging this stranger.

Another medic spoke to the father and directed him and the children back toward the ambulance. The father put the children into his car and followed.

Ann watched them disappear along Abbott Street, with lights flashing and sirens wailing.

As Ann sat again, she thought to herself that it was like she was inside one of her novels. In fact, she realized that her writer's block was solved — she would write this whole event into her story, only it would be a train accident. Still bundled in the blanket that had been wrapped around her, Ann sat while the medic took her blood pressure. She watched everything unfold. The fire was extinguished, the truck was moved to the side of the road, and a tow truck had arrived. A police photographer was busy taking pictures from all angles. It appeared that the truck driver was being taken into custody as she watched him being forced into the back of a police car.

Officer Whalen asked more questions and wrote down Ann's contact information. Time seemed to stand still, like a melodrama playing out before her. The tow truck with Ben's Towing Service painted black against a white body, pulled up to the wrecked car and Ann turned as she heard the officer speak.

"Can I give you a ride home? I don't think you'll feel like running back." He had a big smile on his ruddy face, pleased with his own sense of humour.

"Thanks. My legs are like rubber. I don't think I'd make it."

"Excuse me. Are you the woman that pulled the children out of the vehicle?"

"I'm sorry, but Mrs. Rogers will not answer at this time." Officer Whalen stepped in front of a young man who was obviously a reporter. "A statement will be released by the department in a few hours."

He protectively ushered Ann to his cruiser, opened it so she could sit in the front passenger seat, and made sure she was comfortable. He was particularly careful that he did not touch her injured leg.

Ann saw the reporter point his camera at her.

Following her directions, the officer turned right at Abbott Street and drove to her house. Officer Whalen gave Ann his cell number in case she needed to reach him.

She declined his offer to help her to the house, assuring him she was now feeling in control.

Ray had returned home and was puzzled when he saw Ann being dropped off by the police. He'd been standing on the front lawn when the cruiser pulled up.

When she told him her version of the car crash, he held her tight, kissed her softly and whispered in her ear. "Red or white, my darling hero?"

Chapter 4

Sipping a glass of red wine, Ann was snuggled up to Ray. She was wrapped in a cozy blanket even though it was a warm, sunny day. She assumed that she was still experiencing some shock and that was why she was so cold.

"Nothing like a glass of wine before lunch!"

"Strictly medicinal."

"Ann!" Dan slammed the door as he raced into the house. Dan was her best friend's son who spent fifty percent of his time at Ann and Ray's. It was his second home.

"For God's sake, Dan. You don't have to break the door off its hinges. When are you going to learn to close it properly?" Ray and Ann were constantly reminding him.

"Was that you? I just heard that an Ann Rogers pulled accident victims to safety after a car accident." He took one look at his mother's friend, saw the bandages and knew it was.

Ann had to recount the story again and reassure Dan that she had not been hurt.

Ray eased away, tucked the blanket around Ann and lowered her to a pillow. "I am going to make some lunch. A little nourishment will help you stabilize. Dan, keep Ann company while I rustle up some food."

"What do you mean stabilize? Is Ann hurt?"

"No, but she's experiencing shock. Not uncommon after doing what she did. Flick on the noon news will you please, Dan?"

Dan reached for the remote and hit the power button.

Almost immediately, a picture of Ann being helped into a

police cruiser flashed up on the screen. The announcer was extolling the bravery of "local resident, Ann Rogers."

"Oh crap! Ray? Call Mom. She needs to hear about this before she sees it on the news."

Right then, Ann's cell rang and she saw that it was her mother. She spent the next fifteen minutes calming her and explaining, yet again, the whole story. Dan's cell rang, Ray's cell rang and Ann's did, too, as soon as she hung up from her mother. Brenda called Ray, Li called Dan and friends kept trying to reach someone to hear how Ann was.

"Okay, I think we need to turn off our phones until this settles down."

Dan was deep in conversation with his girlfriend, Li.

The front doorbell rang.

Ray eased into the hallway and peered out the window to see TV vans, cars carrying media logos and, what he assumed were reporters trying to crowd closer to the house. With some insistence, Ray warded off reporters by agreeing to have Ann hold a press conference after the police had issued their statement and information. He then called Officer Whalen and asked if Ann could be sent the release before she spoke to the media. The officer was happy to promise to do so but was adamant that the names of the accident victims were not to be mentioned. Once everything was agreed upon, Ray went to get that lunch he'd started on a half hour before.

"There are reporters on your front lawn." Elsie breezed in, hugged Dan, her self-proclaimed adopted grandson, and headed for Ann. "I locked the door, thought it was a good idea. Honey, are you okay? I am so proud of you but worried sick when I think what might have happened."

"Ray. Someone's at the door. Should I answer it?"

"Go see who it is. If it's a reporter, politely tell them that Ann will be available later."

Dan came back with two huge bundles of flowers.

Ann unwrapped the first bouquet of three dozen red roses, her mother grabbed the card and told her they were from the mother and children, a dozen from each. The other bouquet was a dozen sunflowers from the florist with a card stating, For Our Hero.

Tears flowed down Ann's cheeks. "I'm not a hero. I only did what anyone would have done. This is getting embarrassing."

Elsie set about getting vases and Ray called out that lunch was on the table. Ann had started to warm up and realized that she was famished. The beef broth and garlic bread did the trick.

The doorbell rang again. Dan returned with a large cake box containing a chocolate cake with My Hero on the icing. The card was from their neighbour.

"Well-timed. I didn't find anything for dessert."

Dan grabbed plates, forks and a knife. Stan arrived just in time to share the bounty. He'd been busy in the back yard and hadn't heard about the accident until he went in to get a bite to eat. Elsie had come directly from the hairdresser's and had neglected to call Stan. He ruffled Dan's hair and hurried over to Ann who had once again snuggled under the warmth of the blanket.

Gifts of more flowers, baked goods and chocolates arrived over the afternoon. Neighbours and friends dropped them off, eager to show their appreciation.

"Hey Ann! Thanks for being a hero. The rewards are great!" Dan was tucking into his second helping of chocolate cake. "Did you call Mom? She asked me to have you call. I told her you were busy."

"It's been so crazy, I totally forgot. Can you give her a call and tell her I'm fine? For some reason, I simply cannot get warm."

Ray left the kitchen and returned several minutes later to tell Ann he had run her a steaming bath and asked her if she wanted anything else. The bath was exactly what she needed. Holding the banister, she climbed the stairs to the bedroom. She stripped out of her running gear, throwing her jeans into the sewing basket to be mended at a later date. She climbed into the tub and eased into the bath, carefully lifting her injured leg above the water. With her foot balanced on the tap, she was able to keep the damaged leg out of the water and avoid getting the bandage wet. The bleeding had stopped. The steaming water soaked away any tenseness and in a few minutes, she pulled the plug and eased out of the tub, her skin a deep pink. Finally warm, she took her time to dress with care. Selecting a pair of tailored brown slacks and a cream-coloured shirt, she got dressed then sat at her dresser to apply makeup. She knew that she needed to be presentable and composed for the media.

By the time the police report arrived by fax, Elsie and Ray had organized the living room to accommodate reporters and TV personalities. One local TV journalist had been admitted before the others to help. He offered ideas on how to organize everything for the interviews, then the rest of the reporters were ushered in. When Ann came downstairs, it was to loud cheering and clapping from all the journalists that were now waiting for her arrival.

Dan stood well back with a big grin on his face, his arm around a slight, dark-haired Asian girl with dancing eyes. She wore a short turquoise dress that flared at her knees. Li broke loose and met Ann with a hug and a peck on the cheek then shyly returned to Dan.

"Mrs. Rogers, my name is Arnold Barnes, from CTV. If you agree, I can help field the questions so this doesn't get out of hand. I think the print media should be allowed to go first then we have CBC and CTV here to do personal interviews."

Ann nodded and was led to her favourite chair. A glass of water was placed within reach. She responded with concise answers and smiled for photos. The print media stepped aside and lights were turned on for TV interviews. Ann recognized the journalist from CTV as the woman pulled a chair in front of her. Making sure Ann was ready, she signalled the camera crew.

"I'm here today with not just a local hero, but a celebrity. Ann is a well-known author of women's fiction. She writes under the name of Alice Turnbell. Correct, Ann?"

Ann was not prepared for the direction the journalist was taking and was somewhat taken aback but managed a warm smile as she nodded. The questions regarding the accident went much like the ones for the print media except there was now a blinding light focused on her and the interviewer. Then the reporter started talking about Ann as an author. She was familiar with Ann's work and her questioning was careful and accurate. Ann immediately realized that she was getting valuable publicity.

"Do you think the accident will be featured in one of your novels?"

Ann broke into a broad smile and related that she had been experiencing frustrating writer's block prior to it and definitely had already decided to work it into her work in progress.

After nearly two hours, the reporters left and Ann stood up, reached her arms high into the air and felt the muscles in her back relax. Feeling better, she ran her hands through her hair and went to the kitchen.

Ray was standing there with a freshly poured glass of wine. "My darling, you were wonderful! I wouldn't be surprised if you become a regular on TV."

Stan announced that he wanted to take everyone out for dinner to celebrate this special occasion.

"Can Dan ask his mother to join us?"

Brenda Forest was Ann's best friend, and had been for almost twenty years. They were so close, they were like sisters. They'd met in high school and had bonded and stayed as best friends ever since. Ann watched Dan as he talked to his mother and nodded enthusiastically. When they got to the Brookside Golf and Country Club, they were greeted like celebrities and a bottle of champagne was ceremoniously delivered to their table, compliments of the house.

"Well I have to say that I am overwhelmed by the response of everyone. Many thanks to all of you. Tomorrow, I will lock myself away and write this day into my novel." Ann was brandishing a glass of champagne and her smiling eyes seemed to dance.

Chapter 5

The following week passed in a flurry of interviews and answering tons of emails both in her personal file and her writer's one. The media had played up her novels, which had given her exposure. Sales soared and her agent, Ellen, was ecstatic. She and Ellen had shared highs and lows over the years. This was definitely a high. Ellen managed to get her invited as a guest to two national talk shows and nearly every local radio station. By week's end, the frenzy had died and life had returned to normal. Ann was looking forward to the weekend.

Ray picked up steaks, baking potatoes and salad makings. He wanted a family barbeque hosting the entire family, and included Brenda, and Dan and his girlfriend, Li. As far as Ann and Ray were concerned, they were family. Dan asked Ray if he would be willing to cook Friday instead of Saturday as he and Li were going to Calabogie on Saturday to join a group of friends to bike the extensive trails.

Friday afternoon, Ray unwrapped the steaks and prepared his secret marinade. He smothered the steaks and set them in the refrigerator to season. He scrubbed each potato and sprinkled them with salt and cayenne. He chopped chives and added them to the sour cream. He tossed a huge salad adding fruit and nuts to the vegetables to give it a special flavour and texture. "There, I am all ready."

As soon as he said that, Stan arrived with Elsie. They were both dressed in casual beige slacks, Elsie wearing a white cable-knit sweater and Stan wearing a matching one. He had his guitar slung over his shoulder, ready to strum along with Ray. Stan and

Ray had a special friendship that had grown over the years. Not only were Stan and Ray almost the same age, but they shared many interests, including folk music.

Stan played many old favourites so there was often lots of laughter and zealous voices singing loudly.

Stan and Ray strummed away as Dan and Li danced around the fire pit. The fire's glow soared red then yellow then orange flaring up when new wood was added. The music swelled and faded as the evening wore on into the late hours. Several neighbours had walked around the fence and invited themselves to join in the festivities. Li begged Dan for a rest from dancing and slumped into the empty chair beside Ann.

Dan grabbed Ann and swung her around to a fast number. She swooned and grabbed the arm of a chair and sat down.

"Are you all right? Dan looked at Ann with concern.

"Yep. Just got a little dizzy. I'll be okay in a minute."

"Likely not eating enough protein. The steak'll fix that."

Dan headed off to where the food was and was soon holding his plate out to Ray for a medium-rare steak. He smothered it with BBQ sauce and put gobs of sour cream on his baked potato.

Brenda watched Dan devour his supper, smiling with pride at this six-foot-tall child she had raised single-handed. So often she was almost overwhelmed at how lucky she was to have a son who was never any trouble, chose his friends well and was a good student. She loved his head of blond curls that he wore so long he was always tossing his head to get it off his forehead. His nose was straight, almost Romanesque, and his shoulders were broad. He worked out with weights and ran, so he was muscular and had a ruddy complexion from being a fresh-air fiend. As was often the case, Brenda's chest swelled with pride and love for this young man. She looked over at Ann. Ann was Dan's second mother and Brenda knew that she would not have been able to be the mother she was without Ann. They were a team — not only mothering Dan, but in almost every aspect of their lives. She knew Ann and Ray had decided not to have children so Dan became the shared community child.

As far as Ann was concerned, Brenda got knocked up while on a vacation in Mexico. It was a surprise to Ann when Brenda announced she was taking a two-week break. Brenda never left her business. Brenda owned and operated a concrete and gravel company. Her father was the original owner and had encouraged Brenda to learn the business. Ralph Forest had suffered a massive heart attack when he was in his mid-forties. This tragic turn of events left Brenda broken-hearted, she had been an only child. Her mother had succumbed to breast cancer the previous year. The two deaths left her devastated, but circumstances forced her at twenty years of age, to take charge of the company, long-term grieving was not an option. Brenda had no close relatives, so Ann and Ray became her family and supported her in every way. That was eighteen years ago. Brenda had stepped up and took over the reins of one of Ottawa's largest concrete companies, Forest Concrete. The business was thriving and Brenda was always grateful to her father for having coached her and treating her like a valued partner since she was barely a teenager. This meant that when he died, she had enough training and knowledge to run the company. At first, it was difficult to get the staff to recognize that Brenda was capable of running the industry. Not only was she young but she was small in stature.

It was an emotionally turbulent time and Brenda was grateful for her friends and their support. What she hadn't counted on

Whispers Never Spoken 33

was a brief sexual encounter with Ray. It had started out innocent enough. The week before Ann and Ray were to be married, Elsie took Ann off to a spa weekend and Brenda invited Ray for dinner. This was not unusual as she often did when Ann was away on book-signing tours. When Ray was away, it was Ann she invited. This night however, she broke down and leaned on Ray for support. It was her father's birthday. Ray held Brenda and tried to soothe her as she sobbed and sobbed. One thing led to another and they ended up in bed. Three weeks later, Brenda realized she was pregnant. The hurried trip to Mexico solved her dilemma. She confessed that the wedding and the busy business month had left her needing a holiday. She concocted a story of having been intoxicated one evening in Mexico and that she had been totally bombed and had had sex with a tall stranger, her drinking buddy. She never confessed to Ray that Dan was his son. After returning to Ottawa, she resumed working. Three weeks later, she announced that she was pregnant. Ann and Ray were her constant support and welcomed Dan into the fold as if he were intended to be shared. They were family.

The raucous gathering around the firepit in the back yard broke up in time for the late news. Ann was delighted to see that there was nothing about her on TV. She smiled at Ray.

"I'm heading to bed. I want to get up early enough to get fresh donuts at the bakery on the way to the prison."

"You spoil your inmates." Ray blew an air kiss as Ann left the recreation room to have a shower then settle down for the night.

Ann volunteered at the detention centre teaching English Second Language (ESL), helping inmates improve their reading skills, and working with them to write letters. She spent Wednesday afternoon each week and was devoted to helping, what her family called, her personal inmates. When she first visited the prison five years earlier, the men were less than cooperative. They were restless and often rude — a foul-mouthed rowdy group. Ann persevered and her strong personality soon had them not only behaving, but eager to learn. She learned too. There was no doubt that some of the men had turned to crime because they lacked education. Many were immigrants that struggled with a foreign language. Ray supported Ann's devotion to her charges and often teased her about "her boys". Ann benefited by meeting characters that often surfaced in her novels and she was rewarded by knowing she was contributing to a worthy cause.

Ray, nineteen years older than Ann, was a pilot and often away for days at a time. Ann and Ray had decided, that due to their ages and lifestyle, they would not have children. They knew there were risks to Ray's job and he was often away for weeks at a time. He did not want to be an absentee father. Dan became their surrogate son, almost as close to them as if he were their own. Brenda could not express often enough how Ray was a blessing. Brenda, when she realized the predicament she was in, had simply shrugged her shoulders and accepted that she was on her own. She was strong, capable and turned out to be an amazing mother. As far as Brenda was concerned, her life was perfect — well, as perfect as it could be without her mother and father. Dan was born two years after his grandfather died so had no recollection of him. Ray was the alpha male and played the role well. Little did he know.

Wednesday morning. Ann hurried through the household chores and was about to head out the door when Ray called her to his office. "I just got a call. I have to fill in for a pilot who got hit in the head by a puck at hockey practice. He has a mild concussion so can't fly. I think the flight's scheduled to Paris. I'll let you know. This means I will not be home tonight."

"Good thing you finished fixing the clothesline." Ann moved into Ray's arms and as always, they held each other tightly. It was their ritual.

Ray left the office and returned a short time later in uniform. He was the picture of what a pilot should look like: tall, broad shoulders, narrow hips and salt-and-pepper hair. Ann was comfortable with his travelling with attractive stewardesses and was confident that he would never stray.

Chapter 6

Ann pulled off Highway 417 at Innes Road. The traffic was light so she'd made good time. She arrived at the Ottawa-Carleton Detention Centre and pulled up to the gated entrance. She always had to present her pass to the guard, even though he knew her. Over the five years she had been volunteering, she had been repeatedly admitted by the same guards. However, it was policy that they examine her pass each and every time, even though she was there on a regular basis.

"Nice day."

She was greeted the same every time even though it might be pouring buckets. The gates slowly slid open so she could enter the compound. She always shuddered to see how stark the surroundings were and today they seemed more so with a grey sky and threatening clouds. There were no trees close to the fence and none inside the enclosure. Ann knew this was a security issue, but all the same, she found it disturbing. To her, being surrounded by nature was calming. Having dealt with prisoners for a long time, she knew they were anything but calm. But her role was to teach ESL, not be a therapist, even though she often had her own thoughts about how to help the "boys".

She never knew what prisoner she would be seeing until she was face to face with him. The inmates were chosen based on their week's activities and behaviour. Each one was allotted forty-five minutes with Ann, and she saw three each visit on a one-on-one basis. Due to the aspect of the prisoner's crime, they were considered high risk. A guard always stood outside the door in case there was ever a problem. Over the five-year period she had been visiting the prison, she had worked with over thirty different men.

Ann drove over to her designated parking spot and, once parked, reached for her briefcase and stepped out of her old, dusty, beige Dodge. She realized that her cell phone was still in her purse and would be confiscated at the entrance if she had it with her. Opening the car door, she deposited her phone in the glove compartment. She learned years before not to carry a nail file or anything sharp. Double checking that she had locked the car, she headed for the entrance. As always, she had to walk through the detection device while her purse and briefcase went through the x-ray machine. Once cleared, she was escorted to the small room she always used. It was mandatory for her to wear soft-soled shoes as high heels could be used as a weapon. Her step was quiet as she walked along beside the guard down the grey halls to a green door.

"Saw the news report on your rescue." The squat, burly man smiled and reached for Ann's hand. "I want to shake your hand. Congratulations." Colour rose to Ann's face and she smiled briefly. Once at the entrance to her designated space, the guard went into the room first to check that it was okay, then held the door open for Ann. He was often assigned to her, and she always admired how crisp his pale-blue uniform shirt with the OCDC crest on the upper sleeve always was. The room was windowless but well-lighted with soft, dove-grey walls. It contained two chairs and a table that were bolted to the floor. The guard never left while she was there, and another ushered the inmates to and from the session, one at a time.

A few minutes later, a short, scrawny man about forty-five, and dressed in the requisite orange prison coveralls, arrived and walked to the vacant chair to sit down. He did not raise his head. It was as if he were cowering — until the guard left. When Ann first started working with the prisoners, the guard stayed inside the room, but at Ann's insistence, he was eventually allowed to wait outside with the other guard. Prior to this, she could not get the inmates to relate to her. Ronny had been coming to see her for over three years. She knew he was incarcerated because he had bludgeoned his wife to death. When she looked at this small man in his jumpsuit, it was hard to imagine him being violent enough to commit such a crime, but commit it he had. He was shy, introverted and appeared timid. She knew that many of the criminals housed at this centre were violent and had committed heinous crimes. She hadn't seen Ronny for several weeks. She noticed he had a black eye.

"Well, Ronny, how have you been?"

"Okay, I guess. I wrote another chapter of the book."

Ron was attempting to tell his story and Ann had agreed, if he finished it, she would edit it. She was impressed at how far he had come in the few years they had known each other. He had left school in grade seven to work as a lumberjack in upper Quebec. He was barely able to read, let alone put an intelligent sentence together. Soon after she started working with him, Ann realized that he was dyslexic and introduced the Dyslexie Font to the institution so Ronny and others with the same problem could access it on the computers. Ronny progressed rapidly and became obsessed with reading and writing. Ann had seen examples of his work and knew it would unlikely ever be published, but also felt it was impressive that he'd tackled such a venture.

"So how does the other guy look?"

Ronny glanced at her with a puzzled expression, then realized she was looking at his black eye.

"Believe it or not, I slipped in the shower and landed on my nose. Bled like a sun-of-a-bugger. My eye turned as black as can be. The doctor said I was lucky I didn't break my nose."

"Oops! One can never be too careful but I'm glad it was not a fight."

Her forty-five minutes with Ronny passed quickly and she had fifteen minutes before her next client. When the door opened, she watched a grossly overweight woman about five-foot-five shirk the guard's hand on her shoulder and she shuffled over to the chair and flopped down. Ann had not met this woman before. In fact, this was the first female inmate she had ever had come to her.

"Okay then. I'm Ann Rogers." Ann reached across the table to shake her hand.

"I know who the fuck you are."

"Ah. Yes. Well I suppose you do since you have to ask for this session. Can I ask you your name?"

"Bella. Bella Simms." She spit out her reply in sharp staccato words. Ann couldn't help noticing that her jumpsuit was straining the front buttons and there were already sweat stains showing under her armpits. Even though the woman seemed belligerent, Ann expected she was somewhat nervous.

"Right then, Bella. I need to ask for a few details before we start. This is in order to work with you. Please tell me how much education you have."

Bella lifted her head and her piercing black eyes bore into Ann's blue ones. "Graduated top of my class at Algonquin College. Studied Massage Therapy."

"That's fantastic! Where did you work?" Surprise was written all over Ann's face. One of the many reasons for committing crime was lack of education, and especially, the lack of the ability to read. Seldom did she encounter one with a college degree let alone one that graduated with such high marks.

"Nowhere. Who the hell'll hire an indigenous person to touch their precious clients' bodies? I ended up on the street living in a cardboard box. That's why I'm in here. I killed another street person who tried to steal my locket. It was one my mother had given me before she died. Fucking bitch deserved to die."

"In that case, I can assure you that I will not try to steal your locket."

This brought a snuffled snort from Bella and a small smile. "Yeah, well I can't wear it in here. It is considered unsafe, but I know it's locked away in a container. What are you going to teach me?"

"Your choice. I don't always teach. Sometimes it's about enjoying reading and I bring a book. Or you can bring one to your session. I volunteer to see how I can be of service to you, in whatever way possible. By the way, you are the first female inmate I've had come in. Why did you want to work with me?"

"I saw you on the news. They said you were a writer. That right?"

"Yes. I write novels. Mostly for women."

"Can I read one of them?"

"I would be pleased if you did. I have one here. It's called *After Dark*. Let's start it together and when our session is finished, you can take it with you. By the way, I always bring donuts. Have one."

Ann studied Bella. Her obesity was repellent. Her dark flashing eyes were almost buried in bulging cheeks. Due to her heritage, she had soft, olive tones to her complexion. Ann realized that she must have been a beauty before she put on the excessive weight. She watched as Bella downed the donut before opening the book slowly, almost reverently, and started reading.

"Do I have to read it out loud?"

"Absolutely not, but please feel free to ask anything. And if you wish to continue to read by yourself, that's okay, but I do like to be of some use."

Bella was silent for several minutes, obviously already engrossed in the story. "Is this a real story?"

"Nope. Sometimes the ideas are based on real items, often newspaper articles, but I let my imagination develop the characters and move the story along."

"Have you ever written about indigenous women?'

"No. Mostly, because I have little to no knowledge of their culture to be able to write with any conviction. It's important that I research everything carefully so the reader is not led astray. If I'm writing about a place, I need to know what it's like. If possible, I try to visit it. If I write about a profession, I need to learn about the work the character does and again, I often visit a similar workplace or speak to a professional. To write about someone of a different culture, I would need to learn as much as possible about their lifestyle and beliefs. Frankly, native peoples are very complicated and I would never assume to try and interpret a character of one tribe or another. You could though. You have the inside scoop."

Bella laughed, "No, really I enjoy reading, but not writing. I even dislike writing letters."

"Well maybe that's something you and I can do together, so it's not so difficult for you."

"Hmph. I'll think about it."

When Bella's time was up, she smiled, indicated her thanks for the book, and waddled through the door with barely inches to spare.

Ann took a long drink and thought about Bella as she waited for her final inmate.

She was greeted by a captivating smile from one of her favourite clients. Jorge Hermandez had been one of her first inmates and she had taught him English as a second language while learning a few Spanish words from him in the process.

"Jorge, you look like you just ate the best cherry pie ever!"

"No, Mrs. Rogers. I am just counting the days until my parole."

Ann knew that Jorge had served fifteen years for a gang killing. He was only seventeen when he and three other teens beat a rival gang member to death. He had spent nearly his entire life behind bars.

"Oh Jorge, that's exciting. Do you know when and where you will go?"

"Yes. My mother and my older sister have always been visiting to me. My mother kept my bedroom always for me so I will go home. I be assigned a parole officer and will have to report weekly. I can't wait to eat good Mexican food. My mouth waters to think about it."

"Does the parole officer help you find work?"

"No. I have to do that by myself. My father died while I was in here and my mother doesn't speak much English. My sister not know anything about finding work. She works at nursing home and they do not hire one with criminal record."

"What kind of work will you be looking for?"

"Don't know much about anything except maybe manual labour. I do some yard work here. I seventeen when I came here. Quit school as soon as I turned sixteen."

"You need a verb for a complete sentence. I was seventeen."

"I *was* seventeen when I came here."

Ann had seen Jorge's English improve a great deal, but it was mostly spoken language. She was sure he would not qualify for a desk job. An idea began to filter through her head. She wasn't sure she would see Jorge again before he was released. That being the case, she made a mental note to check something out. His eyes were so dark that one saw only black, but when Ann indicated that she was interested in what Jorge might do once he was released, they seemed to spark. They talked about what opportunities there might be in Ottawa and how he would look for work. The prison would give him some direction and a few contacts that sometimes hired newly released inmates.

"I need find work right away. My mother and sister don't have much money. I need to give them some to pay for my keep."

Ann was pleased to hear his concern for his family and that he was anxious to prove himself. She was also pleased that he had a place to go instead of a group home. Ann explained that most jobs required the applicant to fill out an application form. She showed Jorge some examples of what he might fill out.

"Is good thing to know. Thank you."

The rest of the morning slipped by and Ann gathered up her briefcase and left the box with its two remaining donuts on the table for the guards as was her habit. Before she returned the following week, she would research the new inmate, Bella. The more she knew about each one, the better she was able to relate to them. The prison allowed her access to some records on request.

When she left the prison, she headed over to Forest Concrete to meet Brenda for lunch. She was good and ready for a glass of cool white wine and a slice of Benny's vegetarian pizza. Benny's was a small bistro close to Brenda's business that catered to mostly construction workers but Ann and Brenda frequented it. Brenda's day started early and around lunch time her customers were few, so she often slipped out with Ann. While they were waiting for their orders, Ann changed her mind and ordered a blackened tuna salad and Brenda ordered a cheeseburger. They talked about their day.

When Ann told Brenda about Jorge, there was a pregnant pause in the conversation.

"Brenda, I think he would be a good employee. Would you consider hiring him?"

"Not really. I need a gopher and do-anything kind of guy. And frankly, I'm very nervous about hiring an ex-con, even though you claim he's somewhat different since he was incarcerated at seventeen. Heck. I don't think I could take a chance on him. No, Ann. There's no way."

"He needs a job and I'm sure he would be reliable. Can you at least meet with his parole officer and see if he agrees with me?"

"I could do that, but it would likely be a waste of his time. Ann, look at me. I am a tiny bit over five foot and skinny as can be. I weigh one hundred and five pounds. Convicts terrify me."

"Brenda, he's no longer a convict. He served his time. He needs a break. Please give it a try."

"I don't know. I'd like to help you, but this simply is not my thing. There's no way I'd feel comfortable if he was in the office with me."

"I can understand your reluctance but I wish you would

consider it."

"Perhaps there's a way to have him out in the yard. If I took the yard manager — you know Randy — into my confidence and if he always accompanied Jorge to the office, I might be able to manage it. But honestly, I'm afraid I'd be nervous and never comfortable in his presence."

"I'm sure you'd get over that once you met him. He's really a gentle soul."

"I have a problem with that description. He knifed someone to death."

"Yes, that's true. Keep in mind that he was a wild teenager at the time and was caught up in the frenzy of the moment."

"It's a good thing you're my best friend or I would never consider it at all. You have convinced me to at least give it some thought. Go ahead, arrange for the parole officer to meet with me."

"Oh, Brenda. That's brilliant! Jorge really is a nice man. I'm sure having served his sentence is the only lesson he needed to know he has to work hard and be a good citizen. By the way, he was born in Canada but never really spoke English until he was a teen. That's what he and I worked on when I was at the detention centre. Plus, he's still struggling with written English. Let me see if I can get some information and speak with his parole officer."

"Sorry to cut our lunch short but this is the very reason I need to hire someone. We are so backed up and overworked."

"Leave it with me. I'll see what I can do."

Ann stood up quickly and found she was lightheaded. She grabbed the edge of the table and waited for her vision to clear.

"Honey, are you okay?"

"I just got up too quickly. I'm fine. Get out of here. My treat today. Will I see you over the weekend?"

"Probably."

Ann stood for a few moments longer. Her legs felt unsteady and she was off balance. She watched Brenda leave then gathered her purse and headed for the cashier.

Chapter 7

Elsie had a busy day ahead of her. She had an appointment for a manicure and pedicure then she planned to pick up a special dinner at Palace Regent. Knowing Ray was out of the country, she had invited Ann to join her and Stan for dinner. They would spend the evening playing Scrabble and just plain enjoying each other's company. As she drove to the salon, she listened to the news broadcast. There was concern about a virus that had surfaced in China.

Not letting this bother her, Elsie parked the car and strutted into Beau Belles. Andre greeted her with a bear hug and ushered her to a pedicure station. He presented her with a choice of polish colours. Elsie was in a mood for flare, so she chose a bright coral. Andre left and strutted across the salon looking eye catching in his black smock and slacks. He smiled at each client as he passed them and did again when he returned with a mimosa and tiny éclairs. Andre was the owner of the salon and one of the reasons for his success was that he endowed his customers with special personal treatment. He was in his early thirties, slight with a well-proportioned body, broad shoulders and slim hips. He had a smile that simply glowed, probably due to regular facials that had his complexion gleaming. Even though he appeared feminine, he was far from it. He was a menace on the hockey rink and his three sons were athletic as well. He just knew how to use his good looks and personality to charm clients and guarantee a lucrative business. Once he settled Elsie, he lifted his hand to summon the nail specialist to take over. He gave Elsie a peck on the cheek making her smile in adoration.

Two hours later, Elsie left the salon feeling slightly limp from the massage she'd decided to have as well as her pedicure and manicure. She drove to the East End Mall. She needed a pair of running shoes and wanted to see what new arrivals were at her favourite dress shop. By the time she had visited three shops, her body had recovered and her energy levels were high. The trip was a success as she found shoes and a blouse and skirt — this set her in a triumphant mood. She stepped sprightly along the mall and swung the door open with her hip and almost danced to her car. She tossed the packages into the back seat before getting in herself. She noticed the gas gauge was low so headed over to the gas station to fill up. She was wearing tailored navy slacks and a bulky burgundy sweater. As it was mid-March, winter was gone but a chill was still in the air. While she waited for the tank to fill, she did butt tucks. Never one to waste time, Elsie had a habit of doing little exercises when standing in line or waiting for any reason. At sixty-two, she was trim and still very attractive. She put the nozzle back, being very careful not to get even a drip of gas on her slacks or shoes. Heading home, she sang along with a 50's CD she had popped into the player: "When the moon hits your eye …"

Ann arrived and pulled her car in behind her mother's and grabbed the bouquet of sunflowers she had purchased at the shop next to where she'd bought wine. She could not resist them because her mother passionately loved sunflowers. A soft knock alerted her mother that she had arrived, but Ann did not wait for the door to be answered before she entered.

"I'm here. Hi Mom. Brought you a pressy."

A radiant smile spread across Elsie's face. Holding her arms wide so she did not get flour on Ann's shirt, she leaned over to give her daughter a peck on the cheek.

"Oh, such a treat! They're beautiful! Find a vase under the counter and put them in it for me, will you? I have my hands full right now."

Stan peeked around the doorway. "You gals want a glass of wine?" He raised his bushy eyebrows when he saw the sunflowers. "Oh, lovely!"

Time flew as they tucked into their dinner and Ann praised her mother for getting her favourite dessert of crème brûlée.

Stan offered to clear the table so his girls could get at their Scrabble game. He didn't play the game, so once the table was cleared and the dishwasher started, he wandered off to the den to watch hockey.

Both Elsie and Ann were good competitors and wracked up impressive scores.

"Were you at the prison today, dear?"

"Yes. And the best news is that Jorge is being released in a few weeks and Brenda just might hire him."

"Oh. Do you think that's a good idea? I certainly wouldn't want a criminal around me. Especially one convicted of murder." Elsie was familiar with Jorge as Ann often shared stories of her inmate clients.

"I know, but he's an exception. I think it's a brilliant idea."

"How will Dan like that? His mother helping rehabilitate a man charged with violence?"

"I'm sure Brenda will consult with him before she decides. Mom? Can I ask you a question?"

"Sure honey. Go ahead."

"Did you and Dad want more children?"

"We did. But it just never happened."

"Did you ever ask the doctor why?"

"Sweetheart, this is rather personal. But, yes, we did. It was just not meant to be. Why are you asking?"

Ann watched colour rise to her mother's face. She was obviously uncomfortable with sharing this information with Ann. "Nothing really. I'm going to get another glass of wine. Want one too?" Ann let the topic drop.

"Sure. Never drink alone."

When Ann stood up, she did it quickly and nearly lost her balance. "Oops, I'd better make it a short one for me."

Returning with one full glass and one half-glass, Ann set the full one in front of her mother and the other at her place. "Do you mind if I turn up the thermostat? I'm freezing."

"Are you sure you are not coming down with something? It's really very comfortable in here. And it's not like you to be cold. But go ahead, put it up a notch."

"You know, I might be fighting a bug. I can't seem to keep warm."

"Well take your interfering old mother's advice and get it checked out. When do you expect Ray to get home?"

"Tomorrow or the next day."

Bidding her farewells after Stan announced the news was on, Ann headed home. It had been a long day and Ray would likely phone early in the morning.

The phone rang as Ann pushed the start button on the coffeemaker. She was somewhat of a coffee connoisseur, always buying the best Columbian she could find. She had no problem paying the extra price to get top-rated brands from Jamaica or El Salvador. She reached for her cell with her free hand, her empty mug in her other.

"Hello."

"Is this the sexiest girl in the world?"

"Hah! Haven't had coffee yet and have muggy mouth, so definitely not in that class. How is my best guy?"

"Long day and I'm just tucking into my hotel bed to watch TV. Unlike the rest of the crew, I'm in for the night. We're due for an early departure in the morning and I don't want to be fuzzy headed from lack of sleep, or too much wine. I had a few hours to play tourist this afternoon. God, I love this city. Why don't we pack our bags and spend a month here next fall?"

"Honey! That's a great idea. I'll start doing research. Maybe we can find a little apartment and live like Parisians."

"What're you up to today?"

"Two thousand words. I hope."

"Well, write away. I'll call when I land." Ray had parking privileges at the airport so Ann did not have to pick him up.

"Pizza, beer and a big sloppy kiss await you. Love you. Fly safe."

Ann inhaled the smell of fresh-brewed coffee as she filled her cup. Savouring her first sip, she headed for her office to tackle the chore of completing another chapter of the challenging novel.

Before she opened the file, Ann Googled Paris, the City of Lights. Hundreds of sites popped up. She spent several minutes scrolling through them, selecting interesting information, and dropping it onto a Word document that she then saved to a new file called "Paris".

"Okay, gal. You've wasted enough time and you've finished your coffee." Ann went to the kitchen to refill her mug. Once back at her computer, she opened the file for the latest novel and put herself into writing mode.

Time escaped her when she was writing. Mentally, she became the character or characters she wrote about and entered into the elements of the story. The words came effortlessly for the first time in months and before she knew it, she had written 2,304 words.

"Oh my God, I did it!" She stood up quickly and had to grab the back of the chair until her head cleared. "Maybe Mom's right. This dizziness is happening too often."

She stretched, feeling every muscle that had tensed as she wrote. Grabbing her empty mug, she headed back to the kitchen, checking her cell as she went. Always when she was working, she muted her cell so as not to be disturbed by incoming calls. She glanced at the Missed Calls and noticed a couple but since there were no accompanying voicemails, totally put them down as Robo calls.

"Holy smokes. It's already eleven-thirty and I'm starving!" Ann often talked out loud to herself.

After downing a generous helping of leftover lasagna, Ann headed for the shower. When she was dressed and had dried her hair, letting the soft brunette curls fall where they wanted, she put on eye shadow and liner. She selected a slim, tweed skirt and ivory blouse over which she donned a long, sleeveless sweater.

"Hey, old girl. You'll pass." Leaning close to the mirror, she noticed a few silver strands. "Ah well, I earned those today."

Her cell rang as she was reaching for her purse to go shopping. Before she even had time to answer, her caller was speaking.

"Ann, you have to keep me company. Dan and Li are heading up to Tremblant with a group to do some mountain biking. How about coming over for dinner and an evening of girlie talk?"

"Oh, Brenda, I can't. Ray's due home late this afternoon. So sorry. Let's plan another time?"

After saying her goodbyes, Ann headed for her car. She had several small chores to do and wanted to check on how she could connect with Jorge's parole officer. She decided the best approach was to speak directly with the prison warden. After placing a call, she set up an appointment for 2:40 that afternoon.

"Mrs. Rogers. What a pleasure. I do hope you're not planning to leave us. You have become quite the personality after your daring rescue."

"No, Warden Styles," Ann chuckled. "Nothing like that and for your information, it was not very daring, only busy. No. I've come to talk to you about an entirely different matter. As you know, I've been coming here for five years and have worked with some of the same inmates over the entire time."

"And I congratulate you on your commitment. There's always a long list hoping to be chosen each week. You've no idea what a great service you offer. Now, especially, since you have become such a celebrity."

"Well all the attention has increased book sales, but I do prize my private life and that's why I write under a pen name. My fifteen minutes of fame will pass. Probably by next week. Then everything will get back to normal."

"Please. Have a seat and tell me why you are here."

"Yes, it's about Jorge, Jorge Hermandez. He told me that he is up for release very soon. I may have an opportunity of employment for him. But before I put him in touch with the prospective employer, I wanted to speak with his parole officer and clarify that he would be suitable for the job."

"I'm familiar with this inmate. He served his term well and primarily without incident. He's worked in the kitchen for several years and always offers to do yard work as he likes to be outdoors."

"Now that is good news as this job will likely be mostly out in the yard, in all kinds of weather."

"May I ask what kind of work?"

"Very basic labour. I think it is mostly grunge work, but there's definitely an opportunity to advance. Brenda Forest, my friend, owns the company Forest Concrete and might have an opportunity for him. She inherited it when her father died a few years ago. Although open to discussing Jorge's employment she's reluctant to have an ex-convict on the premises."

"Jorge would welcome physical work. We often encounter reluctance to hire inmates, and once Ms. Forest has met with his parole officer, she may have some of her fears eased."

Reaching into his desk, the warden selected a business card and handed it to Ann. "Frank Hands is the parole officer. I'll have him get in touch with you and he can set up an appointment to visit the job site. That is the first step. Then we go from there. Thank you for taking an interest in Jorge. On a different topic, I noted that you have also seen Bella. She's an interesting case, and I noticed you have asked for her file. If you don't mind, I would like you to consult with her psychologist. She's dealing with some anger issues, but we feel she has potential to learn how to deal with them."

"Sure, no problem. Have her psychologist contact me and we can set up a meeting." Ann was rising from her chair and the warden did so, too. They shook hands and Ann left his office. She knew she had to hurry if she were to pick up the beer and pizza before Ray got home.

Chapter 8

Maneuvering through the garage while balancing a case of beer and a hot pizza, Ann butted the door closed with her left hip. She could feel her phone vibrating in her purse, so she set the beer on the floor beside the laundry cupboard, rushed to the kitchen and set the pizza box on the counter. Seeing it was Ray, she pushed Talk.

"Hey handsome. You landed?"

"Just taxiing to the ramp. Should be home within an hour. Had a beautiful, smooth flight."

"I just came through the door with the beer and pizza, so I'll don my sexiest outfit and wait for you longingly."

An hour later, Ann's phone rang again and again. It was Ray.

"It seems we have a major problem, hon."

"What is it?"

"One of the flight attendants took sick while we were over the Atlantic. Sore throat. Headache. The word from the ground was that we were all to disembark at the farthest exit. When we did, we were met by a medical team in full protection gear. There's a nasty virus circulating across the world and Paris just happens to be one of the hot spots. It's possible that the attendant from my flight is showing signs of having come in contact with it. Therein is the problem. The entire crew and passengers have to quarantine for two weeks. And I do mean quarantine. We are not to be in contact with anybody and that means you. The airline will put us up in a hotel if we can't make arrangements at home."

"Isn't that a mess. Well. Just come home and we will deal with it."

"I don't think you understand, Ann. I'm not to be in contact with you or anyone else."

"That's ridiculous! So what if we get this flu bug? We can sniff and cough together."

"No. Apparently this virus is a killer. And very infectious. I must stay at the hotel."

"Wait. Let me think. Here's what we can do. I can go to Brenda's for the two weeks, and you can be at home. You'll be more comfortable here. Good thing I bought a 24 of beer!"

"This is no joke, Ann. I need you to be out of the house before I get home. Pack a bag and take your laptop. Once I'm in the house, you can't get anything out. All groceries and supplies have to be left on the doorstep to avoid any contact at all."

"But what if you get sick?"

"Then a medical team will determine if I'm well enough to be treated at home or have to be hospitalized."

"Honey. You're scaring me."

"I know. Ann, you need to be scared. We've no choice but to be apart for the two weeks. And if I do get this disease and end up in the hospital, you will not even be able to visit me."

"Okay. I'm trying to understand what you're saying and know I have to deal with this. I guess the main thing is that we remain safe. I'll call Brenda and go there. Once the coast is clear, I'll let you know."

Ann fought back tears as she packed her mid-sized bag and gathered everything she thought she would need for a two-week stay-over.

Brenda's reaction was entirely opposite to Ann's. She was excited at the prospect of having her as a house guest.

Ann texted Ray that she was almost ready to leave the house

and was driving out of the garage as Ray's car pulled alongside the driveway. They blew kisses and gestured hugs as they passed. It was going to be a long two weeks.

While Ann drove to Brenda's, she called her mother and warned her to not go near the house. Of course Elsie thought the whole thing was ridiculous and insisted that she would bake a pie and some bread to take over the next day. Ann strongly ordered her mother to phone ahead and to leave the baking at the front door. She cautioned Elsie adamantly *not* to go anywhere near Ray.

When she got to Brenda's, Ann fired up her laptop and looked up "Coronavirus". The information was alarming. At this point, there were very few cases identified in Canada, but China, where it had originated, was dealing with rampant cases and multiple deaths. News feeds were reporting that it was spreading across the globe. World leaders were encouraging people to limit their exposure to others and reduce social activity. The Canadian government was considering having all travellers from out of Canada quarantine for two weeks upon arrival in Canada.

Brenda came home from work to delicious smells from the kitchen where Ann had been keeping herself busy. They sat down to bulging plates of spaghetti and glasses of Beaujolais, finishing with chocolate ice cream splashed with Bailey's liqueur.

"Oh am I ever going to love having you here for two weeks!"

"I guess we will have to make the best of it. At least I can cook for us."

They rinsed their plates and placed them in the dishwasher, picked up their refilled glasses of wine and settled into the comfort of Brenda's den. The desert-sand walls and the deep brown of the leather furniture added to the warmth of the room heated by a glowing fireplace. Brenda had changed into light-blue sweats and fleece slippers when she came home. Ann was already in denim jeans and slippers, topped with a loose, long-sleeved yellow T-shirt.

"Brenda, last week we talked about the fact that you needed to hire another yard man and I suggested an inmate who was being paroled. Do you still need one? And have you considered Jorge?"

"It's not easy finding someone willing to work for minimum wage and do heavy work. I've interviewed several applicants and they were either awful or refused to work for what I'm willing to pay. My guess is that most of them would hide behind the piles of concrete blocks and either smoke or shoot up. Maybe both. No, I haven't found anyone yet but, a criminal? I don't think so."

Ann proceeded to tell Brenda about her visit with the warden.

"Are you out of your mind? Ann! We talked about this and I will not hire a murderer! I have given it considerable thought. No way. It's unthinkable. And how dare you go behind my back and speak to the warden."

"No, wait. Please reconsider. Jorge was only seventeen when he committed the assault. It was gangland related, a street brawl that got out of hand. He has served his time and has been an exemplary inmate and been incarcerated for fifteen years."

Brenda cut in. "Ann. There's no way. I have my crew to think about and definitely my son. For heavens sake. One of the tools allotted to the crew is a box knife. I'm sympathetic, but not willing to take a chance."

"I know, Brenda. But Jorge is an exception. He's gentle, considerate and I am sure determined to start a new life away from conflict. Brenda, at least give it some thought. I've worked with this man for three years and would never recommend him if I thought there was any danger. He is dedicated to his mother and sister and determined to contribute to their expenses."

"You know, Ann, I am offended that you would even consider proposing to expose me to this criminal. Look at me. I'm a miniature human being. I barely reach five foot, and the scales struggle to reach a hundred pounds. How would I defend myself? If the other employees heard about his record, they would be on the defensive, too, and be unlikely to accept him. This is really annoying to think that my best friend would even consider putting me and my company in such jeopardy." Brenda stood up, turned on her heels and strode away from Ann.

Ann followed. "God, Brenda. I'd never do anything to put you or Dan in danger. Just listen to me for a moment."

"No, Ann. It's out of the question."

"I think you're being overly reactive."

"What do you mean? Overly reactive! Ann, think about it. This man is a murderer. A murderer! He killed someone."

"Brenda. He was seventeen. It was a street brawl. Yes, he had a knife and in the throes of teen anger and frenzy, made a fatal thrust. The man I know, now many years later, is gentle and caring. People change. I know he would work his butt off and be a model employee. As for your other staff, they need not know about his criminal record."

Brenda turned to her friend and stared at her, hostile and angry. Ann's pleading seemed to have no effect. Then Brenda slowly relaxed, reached for Ann's shoulder and nodded.

"I'll discuss this with Dan and the least I can offer you is to think about it. Not promising anything though, as I am certainly not comfortable with it."

The mood between the two friends was tense as they said goodnight and was still uneasy in the morning.

Dan returned late Sunday afternoon. Once he was brought up to speed as to why Ann was staying at their house, Brenda broached the subject of Jorge. Dan's immediate reaction was not what she expected.

"Mom. I think it's a great idea!"

"What? This man is a murderer."

"No. This is about a kid that moved in the wrong crowd and made a big mistake, and has paid the price of fifteen years of his life for one error. He deserves a chance, and you have the opportunity to provide it."

Brenda looked at her beloved son and saw that he was right. She nodded and turned to Ann. "Okay. What's the next step? Not saying I'll change my mind. But I can at least listen."

"I'll contact the parole officer and we can meet with him to get his viewpoint. For all we know, he might not approve your offer. He might not see it as a fit."

Ann left a message with Frank Hand's message service. She received a call from Jorge's parole officer a few hours later. She and Brenda arranged for him to meet and tour the facility the next day.

***

Frank Hands arrived at the office door of Forest Concrete a few minutes early. He took the liberty of wandering along the fenced-in site to get a feel for the operation. He had done some research on line about Forest Concrete. He was surprised that it was one of the largest companies of its kind in the province. Now standing outside the fence, he saw that the area was clean and orderly, which pleased him. He had his back to the office door as he ended a call on his cell and felt her presence before he heard her.

Brenda approached Frank. Walking briskly, she was carrying a file folder and was wearing a welcoming smile. "Hello there, you must be Frank Hands."

Frank turned and was surprised to see a small woman with a big smile.

Brenda reached for his extended hand and her tiny one disappeared in his large palm. "I am Brenda Forest, owner and operator of Forest Concrete. Please come into the office. Ann Rogers is making coffee."

Frank was flabbergasted to learn that a large concrete company was run by this petite, trim thirty-five-year-old. He followed her into the warmth of the office, happy to be out of the raw March morning.

Ann stepped forward to greet him and he recognized her from all the news coverage of the rescue.

Brenda indicated that he take a seat at the round table that he assumed was used for business meetings. The aroma of the coffee and a selection of donuts made him smile to realize that these ladies were trying to make a favourable impression on him. Never one to turn down this kind of hospitality, Frank reached for a plate as soon as he was seated.

"Mr. Hands. As you know, I'm rather well acquainted with Jorge in a classroom setting, but before Brenda can hire him as an employee, she needs to know: one, that it is safe, and two, that he would like the type of grunge work involved and how the system works."

"Well, you are certainly direct and right to the point. You're quite correct on being cautious about hiring an ex-convict. Seldom would I recommend referring one to a company run by a woman, let alone one so attractive and so petite. However, Jorge is the exception. Over the fifteen years he has been incarcerated, he has grown as an individual and I'm confident that with the right kind of support, he'll make it on the outside. That being said, in order for that to happen he will need to receive positive reinforcement and the need to be a contributing member of society. All too often, the transition fails because the convict cannot find employment, and in order to survive, returns to criminal activities. Should you hire Jorge, you need to set clear instructions and expectations. He must report to me every two weeks, and I will do site visits several times for updates. These visits will be random and unannounced. His parole period will extend over six months and then, depending on the results, will either be eliminated or extended. I hope you understand that hiring an ex-convict has its risks. Again, normally, I would not approve this situation except, once again, Jorge is the exception. He has strong family support that's not often the case. Also, the fact that he knows Mrs. Rogers is definitely an asset."

"I understand that his family lives in the area and are anxious to have him home." Brenda refilled everyone's coffee mug. Frank reached for a second donut while nodding his head.

"That too, is a positive situation. Jorge has a lot going for him. Frankly, Mrs. Forest, your offer is exactly what he needs. Mrs. Rogers, is there a possibility that you will continue to coach him in English?"

"Not in a formal sense, but Brenda and I can both see how we can do something to increase his fluency. Also, Brenda has a

Whispers Never Spoken 63

seventeen-year-old son who is willing to help Jorge transition from the prison to life outside. He's a bit of a charmer and may be a little unrealistic, but his influence might be an asset."

"Might we walk the site so you can explain what Jorge would be doing?"

Brenda escorted Frank out the back door. The area was fenced and the office opened onto the site. As Brenda took Frank around the yard, she explained the operation:

"Volumetric and metred mixers are becoming more common. Both types are essentially on-site, custom, concrete plants. Separate holding tanks of aggregate, cement and water are contained in one truck with a computer hooked to augers and pumps. At the site, the customer can order a specific type of concrete — there are more than a dozen — that can be mixed.

"As you can see from the equipment, we are similar to a factory. Scientists in the 1800s began experimenting and perfecting cement, which is what the construction industry still uses today. The name for portland cement came from the Isle of Portland, off the English coast, where deposits of the mineral components used in modern concrete were first found. By 1908, Thomas Edison was experimenting with building pre-cast concrete houses in Union, New Jersey. Most of those houses are still standing and being used. Then there are the famed Hoover and Grand Coulee dams, built in 1936, that stand among the wonders of the world."

She noticed that Frank was nodding approval.

"The mix of a binder, aggregate and water has existed since the dynasties of the Egyptian pharaohs when water, sand and lime were first mixed to use as mortar in building sections of the pyramids. Romans also used a form of concrete in constructing their aqueducts, the Coliseum, and other major constructions."

"I had no idea that cement had such a history."

"The actual concrete has changed little, but the preparation has become automated and computerized. The amount of sand, aggregate and fluid is now measured, and each order is specific to the needs of the job. The measured ingredients move along from the silos — which hold a hundred tons of concrete — to the cement trucks. The Batcher dispenses concrete and prepares the next load at the same time. A huge time-saving operation."

"And all you do is fill cement trucks?"

"No. We enlarged our products to actually manufacturing paving stones, curbs, cement sewage pipes, and we stock enough sand that our construction customers can do one-stop shopping. This is likely where Jorge would start. He would have to learn how to work the loader and excavator."

When they returned to the office, they had reached an agreement to offer the job to Jorge. Ultimately, the decision had to be his. Brenda insisted on one stipulation and that was that Frank was not to tell Jorge that she and Ann were best friends. He would learn that soon enough, but it was not to be part of the reason for Jorge accepting or rejecting the job. Brenda filled out a form and shook Frank's hand. He told her he would get back to her within two days. as Jorge was due to be released in ten days.

"He'll likely want a few days with his family, so let's suggest that he start work mid-April? That will give him almost a week with his family. However, if he decides to work for me, I'd like you to bring him by so he is familiarized with the operation. Should he decide to accept the job, he'll need steel-toed boots, a hard hat and leather work gloves. He'll be on a three-month trial basis after which, if it works out, I'll provide corporate coveralls with our logo. I'll also arrange and pay for a class D driver's licence so he can drive the machinery and trucks. Frankly, I now feel very positive about this decision and have no qualms about his criminal record. Well, maybe a few, but I'm much less worried."

"I, too, have a good feeling about this arrangement. I'm meeting with him tomorrow morning. I took lots of pictures, including some of you, Mrs. Forest, to show him. Hopefully he makes a quick decision and I can get back to you within days."

"It's 'Miss' Forest and do I look forward to seeing you again."

Brenda and Ann stood in the doorway and watched Frank get into a white truck with an Ottawa-Carleton logo on the side panel. He backed out of the parking spot, waving as he left.

***

"Well that went well. I hope I didn't overstep our friendship by getting you into this, Brenda."

"Nope. I am totally okay with this now. Have you talked to Ray this morning?"

"Poor guy is bored to death — bad term. He's climbing the walls and he has only been quarantined for four days. I'm going to pick up some reading material and food. It's so hard knowing he's behind the door and I can't hug him let alone anything else. We have a little routine whereby I sit in the car at the curb and when he comes out to gather his packages, we talk on the cell, wave and blow kisses. So far, so good. He's not shown any signs of infection. Two stewardesses have though, and one is very sick and in intensive care on a ventilator. The national news today announced that in order to curb transmission, all unnecessary services might be locked down. And everyone has been encouraged to wear a mask when out and about. There is also a caution to stay two metres away from others to reduce the chance of contracting the virus. The governments are taking this quite seriously. In the meantime, I'm going to pick up supplies for Ray and a special dinner for you and me. Tomorrow, I have to go downtown to the Central Library to finalize the seminars I am giving there next month."

Chapter 9

Ann was standing on the corner of Sparks Street and Bank talking on the phone to Ray.

"Well so much for planning my efforts and timelines."

Ann watched Ray's facial expression on her phone's FaceTime.

"I parked at the World Exchange Plaza and walked to the library to check out the space allotted for my seminars, and to pick up some reference books. I was informed that due to the new guidelines for the virus, I would only be allowed to have ten people attend my workshops. That really sucks. I have fifteen registered. Now I have to cancel five. What ones I choose will be difficult. Then to top off the morning, I walked to Sparks Street to pick up a travel bag but couldn't find the one I was looking for so decided to head to the plaza to pick up the car and drive over to the Byward Market. I no sooner started along the street than I heard sirens, all kinds of them. I know this is not unusual, but there were so many, it was deafening. Next thing I knew, I was stopped by the police and told the streets in the area were blocked off and I couldn't go any farther."

"Why? What's happening?"

"I talked to the policeman, explaining that I needed to get to my car. It's parked in the World Exchange Plaza. Apparently, there's a bomb scare. And guess where. Yep. The World Exchange Plaza. So my car is trapped and I'm stuck until there's an all-clear. I wouldn't be upset if the old thing was blown to bits, but I don't want anyone to get hurt. Nor do I want the building destroyed." Ann was shouting into the phone to be heard over the sirens and horns and people shouting.

"You certainly can't say your morning is uneventful. What are you going to do?"

"According to the police, it might be a few hours before the area is declared safe. I can't walk east along Wellington. It's cordoned off too. I think I'll head to the National Library and do some more research."

"I'll follow the news to see what's happening. Call me in an hour so I know you're safe."

Ann ended the call and walked west along Wellington Street toward the library. She had been downtown one other time when an alert was sounded. That was one of the drawbacks to living in a capital city. Fortunately, most of the threats were just that, and due to the ability to trace calls, the culprits were nearly always identified. Often, it was someone simply being disruptive. Tourists were terrorized when they experienced a bomb threat, but locals usually shrugged and found something to occupy them until the barriers were lifted.

It was an overcast day and a fine drizzle threatened to turn into a downpour, so Ann was anxious to get inside before she got soaked. As she turned to head west, Ann noticed a large van pull up to the barricades. Two police officers stepped out then opened the back door to allow her to see three dogs. The police officers snapped leashes on them before they allowed the dogs to jump out. Ann expected they were trained to detect explosives.

She was fascinated as the dogs immediately set to work checking along the street. She knew they were known to do a thorough search of the premises and surrounding areas and were often the source of determining when it was declared safe. Everything would be checked before allowing life to return to normal. Realizing that she was getting wet, Ann hurried along

Wellington to the National Library.

Three hours later, the all-clear was announced and Ann headed back to her car. The rain had stopped and the sun cast a warm glow onto the street. Puddles glowed with reflections and rainbow-like oil slicks. She couldn't help noticing how quickly all signs of danger were gone and that everything appeared normal. She hustled south to Queen Street, turned left and headed for the car park to rescue her Sonata.

In no time, she was driving along Riverside Drive and as she was nearing Bank Street, she saw the Royal Swans. There were five swimming majestically along the waterway, their long necks reaching for the sky. Ann pulled to the side of the road, enthralled by them, and seeing them now made her feel that the events of the morning had done an about-turn and the afternoon was going to be much better. She eased slowly forward as it was not safe to stop along that road. She managed to snap a few pictures with her phone that she would post on Facebook later in the day.

Smiling at her good fortune to have seen the swans, Ann continued to Heron Road and drove along to Prince of Wales Drive to her favourite Greek restaurant where she bought dinner for her and Brenda. She decided to get Ray dinner, too, then head to Stittsville to deliver it before going on to Brenda's house.

She let Ray know she was there and after putting his dinner by the front stoop, she waited in her car to see him from a safe distance. "Hey, sport. What's that stubble on your face?"

"I decided not to shave for a few days. Trying to be manly."

"My sweet man, it is not a beard that makes you manly. Sure wish I could put it to the test."

"Saving it up for my favourite gal."

"Sure miss you."

Ann blew kisses and caught the ones sent her way. Ray was often away for days at a time but this was different. She yearned to hug him and be with him but he still had seven days of quarantine left. Countries across the world were reporting elevated numbers of cases of Covid-19, and the general population was starting to become alarmed. Within weeks, governments were issuing directives to wear masks and practise something they called "social distancing". Reports of patients being hospitalized and placed on ventilators, and deaths related to the virus were rising.

Staying with Brenda had been a good decision and they made the best of it. The first night they had snuggled into the large beige sectional sofa wrapped in blankets. Brenda selected a DVD of *Dreamgirls* and they were all nestled in to watch the movie. They sang along and consumed popcorn and wine.

The next morning, after Brenda had left for work bright and early, Ann set up a workspace and planned to get another chapter of her novel written. Before she realized it, it was almost lunch time and Ray would have been trying to reach her. When she checked her messages, sure enough, there were two from Ray. Each day, this became routine, and as Ann wrote, Ray made planters for the garden.

"Six days, six hours to go. I can't wait. But who's counting. God, I miss you." Ray was talking with his mouth full of left-over Greek food that Ann had put on the stoop for him. It was everybody's favourite, so Ann felt it was the least she could do since she was Brenda's freebie house guest.

"At least I'm being productive. I finished another complete chapter and got a start on the next."

"That's my girl. How are you feeling?"

"Had that silly dizzy spell again when I stood up. However, it goes away quickly and now I'm starving."

"Well, eat up and get back at it. Are you there alone?"

"I am. I can hardly wait to hear how Jorge impresses her. He is to have his site visit today. I understand he was excited about working for Brenda, and today he will get to meet Brenda. Dan isn't here. He and Li went for a walk along the canal."

***

Dan and Li arrived back late in the afternoon. Dan quickly let his mother know by text that he was home, attacked the refrigerator, then devoured the last of the Greek dinner. Li had left almost as soon as they got home.

"Is everything okay?" asked Ann.

"Yep. Just famished. Working?"

"Yes. Good walk?"

"The best."

Dan, having swallowed mouthful after mouthful, grabbed his backpack that he had dropped on the floor and with a wave headed for his room. His mother had reminded him that because Ann was working at their house, he was not to play his music at the usual deafening level.

"Isn't this the day the inmate is coming to the plant?"

"I'm anxious to hear how it went."

When Brenda got home from work, she stood at the door inhaling the enticing aromas of chicken soup and freshly baked bread.

"I am going to be devastated when you go home."

Asking about Jorge, Ann and Dan ushered Brenda into the kitchen.

"He does appear to be a gentle, quiet man. He was a bit shy when he accepted the position. Randy took him under his wing, and it seemed to go well. I hope I made the right decision. Let's eat."

Ann returned home after the two-week quarantine was over and other than obeying the safety rules, life carried on much as before. During the months of March to June, the numbers of cases of Covid-19 increased globally and restrictions were implemented on travel, and all group gatherings were cancelled. Ann was disappointed that her seminars were cancelled, and Ray flew only limited flights abroad. He was switched from passenger flights to cargo flights. For each trip, he was asked if there was a chance he had been exposed to the virus, and his temperature was taken both going and returning. On overnight flights away from home, the crews were transported from the airports directly to accommodations, with instructions not to leave the hotels. Upon returning to Ottawa, they had to go right home, but due to the nature of their profession, did not have to quarantine each time they were out of the country. Travellers did.

By mid-March, the world was a different place with public places, non-essential stores, and offices closed. Employees worked from home and families visited virtually. Outdoor activities with proper social distancing were permitted. This was Ann's saving grace as she was able to continue to run.

She did find that her stamina was not up to par, however, and she knew she had not been in contact with any person who might carry the virus. She thought she might take her mother's advice and call her doctor.

"It's not likely anything to be alarmed about, but I will send over a requisition for some bloodwork." Her doctor was limiting personal visits and did most of her consulting by phone. "I'll email the requisition for the bloodwork. You can take it to any lab. Please try to get it done as soon as possible."

Ann followed her doctor's advice. She needed to be fasting, so she made an appointment and went to the lab early the next morning. Traffic was light so she made excellent time driving across town.

When she arrived at the lab, she noted that the entrance was marked with social-distancing markers, and when she entered, she was handed a face mask and queried if she had been near anyone with the virus. After having her temperature taken, a serious-looking Asian clinician told her to sit in a designated area. Chairs were separated at a proper distance to adhere to health requirements. The technicians were masked, and Ann saw that they sanitized their hands before putting on gloves and all the chairs were cleaned with a disinfectant wipe.

When it was her turn, she was surprised by the number of vials of blood that were taken.

"Oh. Your doctor wanted to check out several possibilities. It's not unusual, so don't be alarmed."

Ann relaxed as the technician answered her questions. After the tests, Ann went directly to Tim Horton's and ordered coffee and a muffin. She was famished from not having had breakfast. She planned to write for the rest of the morning so went home and fired up her computer. The storyline was plodding along, but lacked the spark Ann was looking for.

Then feeling chilled, she went to turn up the thermostat but was surprised to see it was reading a high enough temperature. Puzzled, Ann put on an extra sweater and decided to call her mother.

"Hey, Mom. What are you up to today?"

"Your dad and I are driving over to Merrickville to have lunch and walk along the canal."

"Sounds like a plan. It's a heavenly day for it. Be sure to have ice cream. There's no way anyone can go to Merrickville and not have that amazing ice cream. By the way, I did call the doctor and she set me up for lab tests. That's where I spent my morning."

"Good. I'm concerned that you are often tired and feel cold a good deal of the time." Elsie was checking in the mirror for stray strands of hair. She patted a couple into place while she talked.

"Oh, Mom. It's likely some little thing but in today's world, I wanted to get checked. I'm sure I've not been near anyone that has that Coronavirus, but want to have the tests done in any event. Not sure when I'll get results, but whatever they are, I'll be happy to have answers. You and Dad have fun today."

***

Ray had gone on an overnight flight and Ann expected he would be back in time for dinner. Not being sure at what time he would arrive, she bought a selection of foods to make up a grazing platter. She was going to surprise him with the newest David Priest CD she had picked up at the music store. He was Ray's favourite jazz artist. There was nothing they liked better than snuggling up together listening to good music.

Spring was definitely in the air and cherry trees were starting to blossom. The smells in the late morning were soft, and laden with moisture. It was expected to rain before the day was through so Ann had decided to do a late-morning run as soon as she got home. Ray was slated for a four-day weekend so they might plan a few side trips. All the resorts were closed to ward off the spread of the virus, so any outings had to be day trips. Fortunately, they lived in the Ottawa Valley where there were numerous choices of scenic byways. She knew Dan and Li were heading up to Calabogie to go biking with a group of friends, so Ann thought she'd invite Brenda along for one of the days.

She pulled into a deli and bought some cooked meats and desserts. They would pack a picnic because restaurants were now limited to take-out. Once home, she slipped into a jogging outfit and had a good run. When she got back home, she was surprised how tired she was. She had returned minutes before the skies opened up and the temperatures dropped considerably. She decided to spend the rest of the afternoon wrapped in a blanket in front of the fireplace to read one of the mystery novels she'd picked up at the library.

Ray breezed in about seven-thirty and gathered Ann in his arms. "You're lucky to have me this evening. The fog is getting very thick and I almost pulled into a hotel for the night. Then I remembered that the stupid virus made that difficult. So I crawled home and here I am."

"Oh my goodness. Was it a safe landing?"

"Flying is no problem. With the instruments we have now, the plane could land itself. It's driving a car that's dangerous."

"Well, I'm glad you're home." Ann pecked Ray's cheek.

"Hey! Don't I deserve more than that? Here I risk life and limb to get home to my lady and all I get is a peck on the cheek!"

Ann winked and dropped her dressing gown to the floor, revealing that she wore nothing beneath it. Ray eyed the rug in front of the fireplace and led her to it.

Chapter 10

Jorge arrived at Forest Concrete with Frank Hands fifteen minutes before business hours. He was noticeably nervous. Brenda watched this tall, sallow-skinned man with thick, black hair, twisting his cap that he had courteously removed when they came into the office.

After the formalities were over, Brenda expressed how pleased she was that Jorge had decided to work for Forest Concrete.

Jorge blinked in surprise and shuffled his feet. He had expected that he would be burdened with all kinds of rules and regulations. He did not expect that an ex-con would be thanked for what he considered a chance to start his life over. He had not really given any thought to what he wanted to do once he was released, and this was more than he had ever anticipated. To be offered a job right away was unexpected, and he was anxious that he make a good impression. He liked this petite blonde woman who definitely spoke with authority.

"I am thank you for giving job. I do my best for you." Jorge's smile made his black eyes sparkle.

Brenda explained that she had five men on staff, herself, and her son was part time. She did an overview of how the operation worked, and told Jorge that he would be working with Randy Burgess and would take instructions directly from him. Randy arrived right on cue, nodded at the trio in the office, and took his lunch pail to the kitchen. He kept his work boots in his locker so was soon sitting, lacing them up. He went into the office at Brenda's summons. At 6'4" he towered over Brenda and stood a few inches taller than Frank.

"Randy, I want you to meet Jorge. You finally have some extra help. Go easy on him for a day or two. Jorge starts to work on Monday. Could you take a few minutes and show him around while I talk to Mr. Hands?"

Randy grasped Jorge's hand and shook it while grinning with a smile as he ushered him to the back door.

"Poor Randy has been so overworked that Jorge is a blessing. I sure hope this works."

Brenda and Frank went over the necessary forms that needed to be filled out and concluded their business by the time Jorge returned to the office.

"I come Monday." Jorge smiled and did a slight bow to Brenda as he stuck his cap back on his head and followed Frank out the door.

***

On Friday, Dan and Li left early with a bunch of their friends for Calabogie to hike and bike again. They were always on the move. Soon, school would be finished for the year and all of them had summer jobs so the weekend treks would only include those that worked only week days. Brenda was pleased with the group of friends that Dan associated with, and was delighted with his choice of a girlfriend. As far as she was concerned, Li was a real sweetheart.

Brenda was looking forward to the outing promised by Ann. They planned to leave Saturday morning and drive to Kingston for the day and return in time for one of Ray's famous BBQs. All three of them loved wandering the historic streets of Kingston.

Brenda stopped at the liquor store and the bakery and picked up a couple of bottles of wine and a pecan pie. When she arrived at Ann's, she opened the door that slammed shut behind her from a gust of wind and walked right in.

"Hey guys, all set?"

She took her purchases to the kitchen, set them on the counter and wrapped her arms around Ann when she came up behind her.

"Better be one of those for me." Ray was reaching to encircle his second-best girl. Their night of passion was a thing of the past and they were both comfortable with their close friendship. Minutes later, they were on the road. Ray wanted to go via Perth and Westport. Westport lies at the west end of Upper Rideau Lake at the head of the Rideau Canal system. Traffic was light and the skies were clear. Wild cherry trees were in full bloom, and spring was greening everything.

"Crap!" Ray braked, throwing Ann and Brenda forward. He put the car in park and jumped out.

"What the heck is he doing?" Brenda leaned over the front seat straining to see out the window. Ann and Brenda started to laugh as they watched Ray gather up a clutch of turtle babies that were crossing the road. Once he got them to safety, he returned wearing a smug self-satisfied expression.

"Probably should have put the flashers on. I saw them just in time before I ran over them. Ann, can you alert the police that they're crossing here?"

Instead of calling the police, Ann searched for a local habitat group and was lucky to connect with a member. He lived nearby and asked if they could remain there until he arrived. Within fifteen minutes, a battered old Chevy truck pulled alongside, and a broad cheery face waved at them. The rusted door of the once-black truck was thrown open.

"Hey. You are so great! I'll organize enough people to take shifts for a few days."

Ray, Ann and Brenda watched as this large, man with an impressive girth in a checkered shirt emerged from the truck. He placed several signs on the roadside, warning drivers that the turtles were crossing and to proceed with caution. He thanked Ray and the girls before he waved them on with a big smile.

Ray wanted to stop in Westport to check out the camping equipment at Lower Mountain Mercantile. Dan's birthday was coming up in two weeks and he needed and wanted some of the latest paraphernalia that would most likely be in stock there. With easy-listening jazz playing softly on the car radio, the three friends fell into a comfortable silence as they travelled south. When they arrived in Westport, coming off the mountain overlooking the lake, the views were breathtaking. As soon as they were parked, Ray set off on his own while the girls wandered into enticing boutiques. There were signs limiting the number of people that could be in the stores at the same time and cautioning that shoppers had to wear masks.

"Whoa. This virus is sure impacting lives. It must be difficult for business owners."

"I've heard that Paris has a huge number of cases. I hope it stays safe here."

After meeting to eat their lunch under an umbrella on a patio, they headed off again for Kingston. The sun beamed down and there were only a few scattered clouds — a perfect day for their outing.

***

Ray parked the car on Kingston's main street. He considered it fortunate to find a spot so convenient to everything. There were crowds of people wandering along the waterfront and enjoying the trendy shops.

They got out of the car and stretched, then slowly wandered along the historic street, admiring the limestone buildings.

Brenda's phone rang.

"Hi Li."

There was a moment of strained silence.

"What? Oh my God! Where are you? What happened? How is he?"

Ann, seeing her friend visibly stressing, put her arm around her shoulder to offer support, her expression enquiring. Tears ran down Brenda's face and she was gulping air as if she couldn't breathe.

"Brenda. What is it?"

Brenda sucked in air and spoke into her phone.

Ann grabbed it from Brenda's hand. "Li, what's going on?"

Li's responded in a trembling voice. "We were at the top of the mountain when Dan hit a rock. It broke loose and threw him over the cliff. He's lying up against a tree about forty feet down. Todd's trying to get to him to see if he's hurt. I think he is. Oh my God, I'm so scared!"

Brenda, somewhat back in control, retrieved her phone and related what she was being told to Ann and Ray.

"Stay on the line and tell me what's happening. Is your phone charged? Good. Whatever you do, do not hang up. We'll return to Ottawa right away."

"Dan had an accident. He hit a loose boulder and went over the cliff," Ann told Ray.

Brenda returned her attention to the phone. Li was silent for what seemed like minutes when it was only a few seconds. She was watching Todd climb down the cliff, being careful not to fall by grabbing shrubs and boulders. He stumbled a few times, but made good progress. When he reached Dan, he did a quick assessment and yelled up for someone to call 9-1-1. He removed his jacket and draped it over Dan.

"He's unconscious. I think he hit his head. He's alive and breathing, though."

Li related this information to Brenda.

"Li. Stay on the line and keep me informed. We're back at the car and will get to Ottawa as quick as we can. What's happening now?"

About fifteen minutes had passed since Brenda got the call. Li and she kept up a running dialogue with Li explaining what was happening moment by moment. Li was gulping back tears, shaking with fear.

"A couple of the guys are trying to figure out how to get the bike up. It didn't fall as far as Dan so they think they can hoist it up with a rope. Todd is still with Dan. Oh, here comes the ambulance and two police cars."

Ray's car was filled with sounds of sirens coming from Brenda's phone.

Brenda had the phone pressed hard against her ear as if to listen better to what Li described. It was hard to hear above the noise that was going on in the background.

"Okay, it seems the ambulance is equipped to deal with mountain accidents. They are lowering two cables down the cliff."

Brenda related this information to her two friends.

"Two medics are now rappelling down the steep wall holding one of the cables and another medic is attaching a stretcher to the other one to slide down to them."

Li was pacing back and forth peering over the edge to see what was going on. She watched the two medics reach Dan — one set his bags at the ready, the other was assessing how Dan was.

"They're busy with Dan. I don't think he has regained consciousness. I'm really scared."

"You just keep talking to me. What are they doing to him?"

Ray spun out of the parking space, turned on the flashers and raced out of Kingston. He had no sooner got off the on ramp, when he heard sirens. He had no choice but to pull off to the roadside. Once Ray explained to the officer what the problem was, the policeman told Ray he would arrange an escort. He stayed with Ray to Gananoque with his sirens blaring. Here, they were met by another police car that took them as far as Brockville. Yet another led them to the off ramp at the 416 the other side of Prescott. Ray was pleased to see a City of Ottawa police car waiting for them there. It immediately pulled in front of Ray and activated its flashing lights and its whooping traffic warning.

"They have strapped him to a board and are lifting him onto the stretcher. Oh, I hear a helicopter. Yes, it's an air ambulance."

Li watched as the helicopter hovered above the accident scene and saw a pulley being lowered. The medics on the ground attached the stretcher and Dan was lifted into the hold. Without delay, the helicopter turned and was soon out of sight.

Li waited at the top of the cliff as the two medics and Todd were hoisted up by the cables.

The medic who remained with the ambulance approached Li.

"Can anyone give me details about the accident victim?"

Li handed the phone to him. "His mother's on the line."

Brenda gave him the necessary information and learned that Dan was being taken to the General Hospital Trauma Centre. Once back on the phone with Li, they agreed that Li would drive Dan's car and they would meet at the hospital. Her inquiries were readily answered. In the meantime, one medic had loaned the bikers a rope and they hoisted the bike up the slope and fastened it to Dan's car's bicycle rack.

Li came on the line to tell Brenda that Dan's bike looked fine, dented but fine, and that she was leaving the scene and heading for the General Hospital.

"He's being airlifted to Ottawa." Brenda spoke to Ray. "Li did not know how badly he was hurt but insisted that the medics told her he would get the best care at the trauma centre. They also stated that they were lucky he tumbled down the hill instead of being hurled. Li will drive Dan's car home. Oh why did I have to be so far away from home? Hurry, Ray."

"We are just passing Spencerville so should be in Ottawa within an hour."

Li and Brenda kept up a running commentary as Li drove to Ottawa and Ray did the same. Having the police escort was a blessing as they made record time passing everything on the road.

Once they arrived at the hospital, Ray pulled up to the emergency door to let Brenda out. She rushed inside while Ray took the time to thank the police escort then find a parking spot. Then he and Ann went inside and stood beside Brenda as she made inquiries.

Everyone was handed a face mask as a precaution against the

virus that was becoming a concern and spreading rapidly.

Li rushed in right then. She was flushed and her face was streaked from tears. Her long black hair was disheveled, and her cycling shirt was damp with sweat. She wore black pants with red slashes down the thighs and a long-sleeved matching jacket. Everyone embraced her and told her they had been informed that a doctor would be with them momentarily.

"It was scary as hell. I was right behind Dan when he went over." Li was crying as she talked. "It all happened so fast. He tumbled about thirty or forty feet and a tree stopped him from going all the way to the bottom. Todd scrambled down and told us that Dan was unconscious but alive. He said he thought Dan was seriously hurt. One of our friends called 9-1-1." Li was speaking rapidly and took a big breath. Ray handed her tissues to blow her nose. "There was nothing we could do until the helicopter arrived. It was so scary." Li was so flustered she didn't realize that she was repeating what she had already told Brenda on the phone.

Ray gathered Li into his arms to quell her shaking. He looked up to see a doctor approaching them along the corridor. The bland, beige halls were crowded with people milling about. Apparently, there had been a serious car accident involving four injured people and at the same time an ambulance had arrived with a stroke victim. The hallway was noisy with people holding each other, leaning against the wall, or sitting in the few chairs that were provided. Smells of sweating bodies were mixed with antiseptic and disinfectant odours.

"Mr. Forest?"

"No. His mother is Brenda Forest." Ray indicated Brenda.

"Dr. Hasad." The doctor extended his hand to Brenda. "Your

son has had a nasty fall and is in recovery. He has a concussion, a broken arm and three fractured ribs. He will be one sore young man for a few weeks. We'll keep him in hospital overnight then he'll have to undergo physiotherapy for several months. I'm afraid his biking trips will be cancelled for the rest of this year."

"How soon can I see him? Is he conscious?"

"He's being moved to the ICU. Once he's settled, you can go in, but please be prepared to see a very bruised and pale son. Only you and you husband will be permitted in the ICU."

"I'm a single mom but Li is his girlfriend, can she come?"

"We can make an exception in this case." Dr. Hasad shook Brenda's hand again, nodded at the rest of the gathering before he turned to leave.

A wail went up from one of the people waiting in the chairs. An elderly woman was obviously distressed at receiving news from someone bending over her. A young man knelt at her side and cradled her with his arms around her shoulders.

Brenda paced the floor, wringing her hands. "Thank God he was not alone. Do you know how often I chastise him for biking on his own? Li, stop blaming yourself. You did all the right things. Now we'll have to deal with a very impatient and grumpy patient. I do not relish the months ahead. I know he'll be impossible."

Ann smiled at her friend. "We're here to help. Whatever you need, just ask. Technology might save the day. Thank goodness for computer games."

Everyone laughed, the tension eased somewhat now that they knew Dan had only to recover. It was now a matter of waiting until Brenda and Li were given permission to see Dan.

Ray went to the cafeteria and brought back drinks and a

sandwich for Li. She had not eaten since breakfast, and it was nearing the end of day.

Once Brenda and Li were allowed in to see Dan, Ann and Ray waited for them in the crowded hallway. Ann noted all the comings and goings thinking how she could write what she was witnessing, how she could bring the scene alive with words. Words ran through her mind as she searched for the right ones to express the agony she saw on waiting people's faces, the relief on others' and the boredom of some. She'd already written in a train accident, and now she had ideas of how to record the trauma centre to which the characters would be taken.

Brenda's and Li's visit was limited to a few minutes. Tears rolled down Brenda's face when she saw how pale Dan was, with tubes running from his nose. She stroked his forehead and lifted her eyes to the ceiling. "Thank you." It was a sincere prayer.

The nurse in charge of Dan's care told Brenda and Li that Dan would be roused regularly but would not likely be aware of having company.

When they returned to Ann and Ray, both Brenda and Li had tear-streaked faces and feeble smiles.

"He looks terrible."

"I expect the bruising will be worse tomorrow but we're fortunate that he was not killed."

Ray gathered Brenda in his arms and gave her a big hug. Ann did the same with Li.

As they turned to leave, they followed the distressed family to the door. Ray pushed ahead to hold it open for them. The old lady was leaning on the young man for support wailing loudly.

"But for the grace of God …" Ray murmured.

Ann drove to Brenda's. Ray drove Li to her house in Dan's

car, off-loaded her bike from the bicycle rack, gave her a hug and promised to call her if there was any more news.

Once Li's bike was removed, Li indicated that she was able to manage. "I'll call the others — our friends that were with us — and let them know how Dan is."

She and Brenda had agreed to keep each other informed as to Dan's progress. Li would pass along the information to everyone concerned and no doubt post the news on Facebook.

Ray stopped and picked up a pizza and a bottle of wine and drove to Carp where Brenda lived.

Ray was brandishing the pizza box over his head as he stepped out of the car. When he crossed the threshold, he tripped and nearly lost his footing almost dropping his precious cargo.

Ann let out a loud hoot and bent over double as she laughed at Ray. The ridiculous scene brought a smile to Brenda's face. "God, Ray. You always can steal the scene. Come on. I need to sit down and plan how to manage the next few days."

"Ray and I can be here to help during the day while you're at work. I know this is a very busy time of the year for you and I believe Jorge starts work Monday?"

"Oh God! I forgot about that. I hope I can concentrate by then. You know, I'm still nervous about hiring a murderer."

"You have to get past thinking that and accept him as a person, an employee. Not an ex-con. Have you met him yet?"

"Yes. He came by with Frank Hands."

Brenda sprawled on a kitchen chair and stared into space. "My life is a fucking mess!"

Ray came up behind Brenda and started massaging her neck. He stopped and pulled up his grey sweatshirt sleeves and resumed massaging. Ann gathered plates, napkins and wine glasses and set them in the centre of the table.

"Wine first. We need to loosen up all this tension in the air."

She poured generous servings and slid into the chair beside Brenda, giving her a kiss on the cheek as she bent. "You know, I write about the challenges my main characters always face, never expecting to be caught up in our own drama. Here." She handed each a glass of wine. "We are experiencing real life ventures."

Before leaving Brenda, Ann and Ray made sure she was calm and ready to face the next day. Brenda assured them she would try to get a good night's sleep — even though it was unlikely.

Chapter 11

The next few days settled into a routine of sorts as Ray and Ann drove to Brenda's, arriving as Brenda left for work at 6:45 am. Dan had come home by ambulance late Sunday afternoon. He looked worse than he felt, although all he wanted was to stay in his bed and sleep. Brenda checked on him every hour all night. By morning, she was exhausted but knew she had to go to the office.

Dan was not yet awake when Ray and Ann arrived, but Brenda felt better having someone there. Happy to reassure her, Ann had no problem giving up her morning run and Ray did not have any flights scheduled until Thursday. Ray was invaluable as he could help Dan do the bathroom routine, and shower and dress.

"Okay, champ. Time to rise and shine." Ray was leaning against the door frame of Dan's bedroom at nine o'clock. "Do you want breakfast first or hit the shower?"

A muffled sound came from beneath the brown duvet. A tussled head appeared and Dan gave Ray a look that would sour milk. "Go away. I hurt. I don't want to get up. Go away. Leave me alone." Dan disappeared under the covers again.

"Not going to happen. I know you must be very uncomfortable but the more you move around, the sooner the muscles will heal. And besides, your medication has to be taken with food."

"Don't care."

"Either you make an effort to get up on your own or I'm going to drag your sorry ass out onto the floor."

"You are one mean son of a bitch." Dan peered from under his covers then slowly eased his foot out and pulled it back when he felt the cold air. One look at Ray's face and Dan squinted his eyes in the most evil expression he could muster, then made the ultimate effort to get up.

With each movement he groaned and Ray winced, feeling each pain with Dan. He knew everything hurt. As Dan slowly emerged from beneath the covers, Ray was dismayed to see how bruised his face was and noted that Dan's nose was very swollen.

With a great deal of effort, Dan managed to sit on the edge of his bed. He bent over trying to concentrate on breathing shallow breaths so his ribs didn't hurt so much.

"Is it hard to breathe? Yeah, well, broken ribs will do that. Your nose is a bit of a mess, too. Can you stand on your own or do you need help?"

"I need to go to the bathroom and I definitely need help. Dizzy as can be."

Ray helped Dan stand and gave him a soft hug for support before he lifted Dan's good arm around his shoulder and was able to bear Dan's weight. When they got into Dan's bathroom, they ended up in a fit of giggles as Ray tried to support Dan and, at the same time, get his pajamas bottoms down.

"Okay. This is not working. Lean on the toilet tank, for God's sake, or you're going to end up on the floor."

Dan was able to rest his good arm on the tank lid as Ray dealt with the pajamas.

"Hey. I can't point and shoot at the same time as I'm holding the back of the toilet."

Ray wrapped his arms around Dan's waist so Dan could manage peeing, then between the two of them, managed to get the pajama bottoms up and Dan turned around.

"So help me, who ever thought we would be doing this? You're lucky I didn't pee all over the floor and you'd have to mop it up." Dan tried to laugh but stopped quickly when he realized how much it hurt, how sore his ribs were. He did do a semblance of a snort, a sort of laugh that was more of a giggle.

They were still giddy when they got to the kitchen.

Ann had prepared scrambled eggs, bacon and toast. She turned to see the men arrive and stood stock still when she saw how damaged Dan was. She put her hand over her mouth with dismay as she watched Ray guide Dan to a chair. Ann shook her thoughts free and served the plate she had been holding.

Once seated, Dan was able to eat on his own with his one good arm doing all the work. He gratefully accepted the painkillers Ann handed him with a large glass of milk.

"You know, just the effort of eating has used me up. I'm exhausted. Can I have my shower later?"

"Let's try to get it done now. I know it is difficult, but I need to make sure the cuts and scrapes are cleaned."

"How will I be able to have a shower with my arm in a cast?"

"I broke my arm when I was twelve years old. My mother bagged it in a garbage bag, taped it on, and it worked very well to keep the cast dry."

Ann leaned down from the sink where she was rinsing dishes and reached inside a box and handed Ray a green garbage bag. "There's tape in the medicine cabinet in Brenda's bath. I'll get it."

When Dan was showered and dried, Ray helped him back to bed. The painkillers were taking affect and Dan simply snuggled down and was fast asleep within minutes.

"Oh, Ann. That poor boy is bruised and scraped nearly all

over his body. I swabbed the scrapes and dressed the open cuts. The doctor is coming by later, I understand."

"Actually, it's a nurse practitioner. I think they're coming about ten-thirty."

At 10:30 on the dot, the buzzer announced a visitor. Ann opened the door to a tall, black man who towered over her. He was dressed in casual beige slacks and a white T-shirt with a small logo indicating that he belonged to the MOP, the Medical Outreach Program.

"Hey, I'm Fergus. I understand you have a fellow that took a dive down a cliff."

Ann laughed and ushered him into Dan's bedroom. Dan had been awake for about half an hour, had visited the bathroom again, and was now propped up in bed on pillows.

Fergus introduced himself and explained that he would be assisting with all Dan's healing needs for months to come. "We're going to become either great friends or absolute enemies." Fergus pulled the blankets down, lifted away the pillow and with his arms around Dan's waist, hauled him down the bed until he was lying flat.

"Crap, that hurts!"

"I'm sorry, but I have to do what I have to do."

Fergus explained that first and foremost, the bruising had to be dealt with. He pulled a large pad out of his bag, then another. "Missus, will you please microwave this for several seconds?"

Ann took the pad and took it to the kitchen. Ray watched as Fergus lay the other one over a large bruise on Dan's left leg.

"Damn! That's cold! What are you doing?"

"We will alternate between cold and hot to get the blood moving. This avoids clots forming. This bruise is very deep and will take a few days to start healing. Frankly, if your mother can continue to do this several times during the day, it will hasten the healing."

Fergus left the cold compress on Dan's leg for about twenty minutes. Ann returned with the heated one and the same process was administered with that one.

"The heat feels better."

In the meantime, Fergus massaged the uninjured arm, Dan's neck and feet. He spent about an hour with Dan and informed him he would be back the next day. He left the compresses with Ann so she could freeze one and heat the other. She made notes for Brenda, then made lunch. She set a help-yourself platter in the centre of the round oak table. Brenda had found it at a salvage yard and had stripped and refinished it.

Fergus helped Dan into the kitchen with instructions to move as much as he could stand to.

"Would you care to join us for lunch?

"No thanks. My next appointment is clear across town and I have packed a sandwich to eat on the way. Dan, it's a good thing your mom and dad are here to help you." Fergus was easing Dan into a kitchen chair that Ray held out for him.

"They're not my parents. Well, not really. Might as well be, though."

Fergus left with a puzzled expression on his face.

Ann made tea for her and Ray and placed a large glass of milk in front of Dan.

"I don't remember falling. It all happened so fast. I do remember hitting the rock on the trail, though, and thinking I was in trouble." Dan spoke between mouthfuls.

"It didn't hurt your appetite."

Once lunch was finished, Ray helped a very tired Dan back to bed. When Ray returned to the kitchen, he helped Ann with the dishes. "It's a good thing he can sleep. He'll heal faster that way."

Li arrived shortly after 2:00 that afternoon and Ann and Ray left her to visit with Dan.

They were soon playing a video game on his laptop.

After about two hours, Li came into the den where Ann and Ray were watching the early news.

"He wants to sleep. I'll come again tomorrow. When he fell off the cliff, I was terrified he was dead. I hardly slept last night and when I did doze off, I would awaken shaking and crying. This visit did both of us a lot of good. I just wish there had been something I could have done to prevent him going over the cliff."

"You did all the right things, my dear. Because you acted so quickly, and were so efficient, he was rescued and received care as soon as possible. He's one lucky guy to have been with you and your friends. If he had been on his own, he likely would not have survived. That is one of the reasons Brenda insists that he always ride with company."

Brenda arrived home as Li was leaving. Ray poured himself and his girls a glass of wine and Ann filled Brenda in on the day's happenings. They assured Brenda that it was no trouble to be there the next day. Ann was anxious to hear how Jorge made out his first day.

"He was really early and was waiting out front when I arrived. I have no idea how long he'd been there. He's very polite and stood by Randy in order to see how the operation worked. He basically stood aside watching. Randy did give him a few easy chores. Being the beginning of the week, we were quite busy. Once the morning rush slowed down, Randy gave him some lessons and kept him busy. Seems he was doing fine. I didn't really pay much attention. Left him to Randy. I was in a hurry to get home to you guys and Dan. How is he?"

"He's coming along. Li dropped by, as you know, and earlier the nurse practitioner worked with him for about an hour. He is exhausted by the least little effort so slept a lot. Thank God for Ray. Dan couldn't have managed the toilet needs without his help. I'm sure he was glad it was not me holding him as he did what he had to do." Ann was leaning on the white marble countertop smiling at her best friend.

The following afternoons were busy with Dan's friends dropping in and by Thursday, Dan was able to manage on his own so Ann came alone as Ray had a flight scheduled.

Brenda still had reservations about Jorge but had to admit he was a good worker and got along well with the rest of the crew. On Friday morning, Ann left Dan with Li and had dropped by Brenda's office to entice her to escape for a couple of hours of girl time.

"Not going to happen today. I'm so busy. It's insane."

They were looking out over the yard that had several cement trucks, four half-ton trucks and two flatbed carriers all in different parts of the yard, loading up for the day's work. Every morning between 7:00 AM and 8:30 AM, it was a scramble to fill the orders and make sure everyone's order was being filled to exact specifications. However, it was extremely busy and at 10:45, the yard was still full of customers. The hopper was filling a truck with cement that Brenda had programmed into the computer. She had a few free minutes while it was filling to spend with Ann but little else.

"Our boy, Dan, is getting about quite well now. I expect he'll be able to help me here in the office in a week or so. No lifting or heavy work, but he can program the computer and do some paperwork. I can't thank you and Ray enough for your help."

"It's a good thing his studies were finished for the year and he had finished all his exams."

"Dan and I talked about that, and we're pleased he didn't have to deal with studying at this time. His results should be released soon."

Brenda watched a concrete truck leaving after filling up at one of the huge silo-like hoppers and was waiting to get around another client's truck that was picking up patio stones and another getting loads of sand. The yard was alive with activity. All of a sudden, Brenda saw Jorge race across the yard and tackle Randy throwing him into a pile of sand.

"What the hell? I knew I couldn't trust that damned convict." Brenda was on her feet racing to the yard.

Ann followed.

"Holy shit! Did you see that?" One of the truck drivers had slammed to a stop and was running toward Jorge. "Man, you saved Randy's life. Here. Take my hand." He helped Jorge up from lying splayed across Randy.

"You okay, Randy?" Jorge was breathless.

"What the hell happened?" Brenda yelled to one of the men as she crossed the yard.

"One of the large concrete pipes fell off the pile when the Ottawa maintenance truck backed into the stack. Shook it loose. Those darn pipes weigh nearly three thousand kilos. Man! It dislodged and rolled fucking fast toward Randy. He had his back to it and had no idea he was in its way. With all the activity in the yard, he wouldn't have heard it either. It would have killed him if Jorge has not thrown him into the dirt. The pipe missed the two of them by inches."

Brenda stood catching her breath, bent over with hands on the knees of her green coveralls.

"Hey, Brenda. Don't deduct my pay for the sand I swallowed." Randy eased upward, balancing his weight on Jorge's shoulder as he brushed his coveralls free of sand. Both men looked at the now-motionless concrete pipe that had come to rest up against one of the maintenance sheds.

Randy turned and gave Jorge a big hug. "Thanks, man. I owe you one. That bugger would have squished me flat. I could do with slimming a bit but not that way."

Both broke into nervous laughter.

Jorge blushed, his tawny skin flushing darker.

Brenda, now aware of the situation, quickly went up to Jorge. "That was one quick-thinking thing you did. I wasn't sure what was going on, but now that I do know, I want to say how grateful I am that you acted so quickly." She took Jorge's hand and shook it.

Ann was standing behind her, watching.

"Mrs. Rogers, what are you doing here?" Jorge was staring at Ann, not comprehending why she stood there.

"Come into the office and I'll explain." Brenda was now aware that the cement truck that was filling at the silo was finished and had left the filling station. She watched another moving in to load up. Randy was already back at his job, signalling the driver so the truck was perfectly lined up with the loader. Brenda had to get back to the computer to program it for the right strength of mix as noted by the client. As soon as she got to the office, she noted the request, typed it into the computer and hit the "Go" button when she saw Randy signal that the truck was attached properly.

She turned to Jorge.

Ann was handing him a cup of coffee.

"Mrs. Rogers is the one responsible for me hiring you. You see, Jorge, you didn't know it, but Ann and I are best friends. She pestered me until I finally gave in and agreed to take you on. I was very reluctant to do so knowing your history. After this morning, I take every negative thought back and I want you to know that welcoming you to Forest Concrete was the smartest thing I've ever done. Enough praise, finish your coffee and get back to work. Randy is already hard at it since this morning is crazy busy." Her smile glowed across her entire face; she was shaking and shaking Jorge's hand.

"I don't understand. Why would Mrs. Rogers recommend me?"

"Jorge, you and I have worked on your literacy for several years. I think I became very aware of the man you are. I believed in you and wanted to help. After what you did today, I'm sure glad I did." Ann was smiling and nodding at a dumbfounded Jorge. He returned her smile, set the still-full coffee cup down and modestly slipped out of the office to the yard.

Brenda went over to Ann and gave her a crushing hug. "That man not only saved a fine man and a valuable employee but in all likelihood, it could have been a very costly libel suit. Excuse me, Ann, while I go out and direct the crew to place barriers along the pipe stack. There's always something. I know you wanted to go shopping but, as I said, not possible. Now I'll have to have a staff meeting as soon as the morning crowd disperses. Probably by eleven-thirty or so I can get away for lunch?"

"Brenda, I don't know how you can be so calm. I am still shaking. I'll go and pick up some things I wanted from the nursery then come back."

Chapter 12

When Ann returned, she and Brenda set off to Bayshore Shopping Centre where they planned to have a quick lunch and take a look at what was on sale and what was new. With fresh spring stock in nearly every store, there was lots of temptation. Ann turned and went straight into the nearest shoe store right away with Brenda tagging close behind.

Brenda held up a pair of sling-backs with five-inch heels. "I have no idea how women balance on these things. It's like wearing a deadly weapon on your feet, not only dangerous walking, but truly a dagger heel."

"I could use— Whoops. I need to sit down." Ann slumped onto the nearest bench and put her head between her knees.

"Ann. Are you okay? Well I know you're not, but what just happened?"

"I suddenly felt really faint. This has happened a couple of times in the past few weeks. It passes quickly. I'm fine now. Nothing to be concerned about. Mom thinks my blood might be low. She's probably right. Doctor Burns sent me for blood tests. The technician took enough vials of blood to empty my arm. No doubt the doctor will prescribe some nasty iron supplement. Come on, I still need a new pair of sandals." Ann was on her feet and walking rapidly across the court.

Brenda stared after her friend with concern. She watched Ann's long legs carry her off looking elegant, even in her casual wear. Ann was always impeccably dressed, definitely something she acquired from her mother. As long as Brenda had known Ann, she was always healthy and full of energy. This light-headedness was something new.

With shopping bags at their feet, the two friends sat in the food court sipping lattes. Brenda had hung her pale-blue spring jacket over the back of her chair commenting how warm it was. She had shed it nearly as soon as they got inside the mall. She wore a light, long-sleeved pale-blue sweater and grey jeans with jewelled studs on the pockets. "You must be roasting. Why don't you take off your coat?"

"Actually, I find it chilly in here." Ann was wearing a suede buff-coloured jacket, brown jeans and running shoes. They were chatting away watching the crowd on the lower level and commenting on what they saw. "I think that top you bought is stunning. It will go so well with those blue pants that you're always complaining that you have nothing that matches."

Ann's phone rang.

Seeing that it was the doctor's office, she held up her hand to Brenda before answering. "Good. Now maybe I will have an answer to what is causing this silly dizziness. Hello."

Brenda watched as her friend listened to the phone call. Ann's face changed from relaxed and smiling to one with a worried expression. Ann ended the call and looked at Brenda. "The doctor wants me to get some more blood tests, something about the last batch being inconclusive. God, they took enough. Oh well, as long as they get to the bottom of this. I sure don't like this stupid dizziness. They want me to fast again and the doctor wants me to go tomorrow morning. At least she's taking this seriously."

"Listen, Ann. I have to dash. I've been away from the office far too long. Let me know what's causing this light-headedness as soon as you know. Bye now. See you." Brenda leaned over and air-kissed her cheek, turned, and was soon well down the mall.

***

The next morning, Ann leaned over Ray, who was still in bed, and gave him a peck on the forehead. "Off to the vampires."

A muffled "Mmph" answered her.

Like the previous visit, she was masked and set apart from other people waiting for their turn. She looked around her to see there were three other patients waiting. An elderly gentleman wearing a navy jacket sat with his peaked cap on his knees. There were no magazines for clients to read, so Ann was making mental note of how the other clients looked. This was a habit she had so she could transfer the information to her writing. One heavy lady in grey sweats and burgundy sweater rose and. using a walker. went to the booth that the technician had indicated. Ann was called next. Once again, the technician took several vials of blood and requested a urine sample as well. After the session was over, Ann headed right for the coffee shop and treated herself to a raspberry muffin and a latte.

"Ann Rogers, is that you?"

Ann looked up at a tall, large-boned woman towering above her. Ann had guessed her presence before she heard her. There was no question as to who it was. She always had a slight aroma of horses about her.

"Hey, Kim. Sit down. How are you? It's been months since I last saw you. My goodness, you look amazing. What's new?"

Kim Noble took the seat across from Ann, set her coffee and donut on the table, and leaned over with her arm outstretched. Ann was puzzled until, after some elaborate hand wagging, Ann noticed a large diamond flashing on Kim's finger.

"Kim! When did this happen? And what is more important, who is he?"

"Listen, at forty-three, I never thought I'd find Mister Right, but not only did I, he is tall. I need that. And handsome and charming and rich. Can you believe that? Boris moved here from the Ukraine to breed horses. We met at a barrel competition. How perfect is that?"

Kim was not overweight, but she was a big woman, tall and big-boned. Whenever, which was seldom, she was not wearing riding gear, she always wore the latest fashions. She had her soft, curly, auburn hair dressed in a short cut and her complexion was permanently tanned from being constantly working outside training and grooming horses. Today, she was radiant.

"Wow, Kim! I can't wait to meet him. We'll have to have you both over for an evening. Ray's home a lot these days with this virus making travel limited."

"Nothing I'd like better. You will love Boris. And I do want him to meet my friends. What on earth brings you to this end of town?"

"Oh, just some routine blood tests. I was at the vampire clinic."

"Listen. Let's try to get together next week. I haven't seen Brenda for ages, either. I have to dash, but give me a call and let's plan that evening." Kim had swallowed her donut and swilled her coffee in what seemed like one gulp.

Ann watched Kim ease past several people trying to enter as she was leaving. Kim, Brenda and Ann had been steadfast friends when they were younger, but with Kim living in the east end, and Ann and Brenda in the west, Ann in Stittsville and Brenda in Carp, they seemed to drift apart. Their lifestyles and careers were vastly different, but regardless, there was still a bond. Time had escaped the three and when Ann thought about it, she realized that it had been over eleven months since she'd spoken to Kim.

Ann picked up her phone to call Brenda then realized that it was her busy time of day. She made a mental note to call later and tell her all about running into Kim.

When Ann got home, she switched on the local news and listened carefully to the reporter giving details on the spread of the Covid-19 virus. Governments were urging everyone to wear a mask and stay away from others if possible. The number of cases was starting to be alarming and the numbers of deaths rising. There was talk of shutting down businesses and community facilities. Ray's one co-worker was on the mend, but the other one who had been hospitalized and in intensive care for over a week on a ventilator, apparently was slowly improving. The reporter emphasized that seniors were very vulnerable. Ann made a mental note to talk to her mother and father about being extra careful.

Later in the day, Ann phoned Brenda. "You will never guess who I ran into today."

"Not a clue."

"Kim. Kim Noble."

"For heavens sake, how the heck is she? I haven't seen her for months."

"Are you sitting down? She is sporting an enormous diamond on her ring finger."

"Real or fake?"

"Real. And she says she landed a great match complete with money."

"No! Wherever did she find a prize like that?"

"At a horse event. According to her, he is tall, handsome, charming and very rich."

"Like I can believe that!"

"Well, her idea of tall, handsome, charming and rich might not be the same as our interpretation. Anyway, she's very happy and wants us to get together and meet the love of her life. I thought we could do a dinner next week. Are you game?"

"Of course. There's no way I'd miss that! You have piqued my interest. Now I have to see this guy."

"One thing I can share is that he is a horse breeder. Oh, and he's Ukrainian."

"Oh great. We'll likely have a lot of trouble understanding him with his heavy accent. Plus, the entire conversation will likely be about horses. Oh well, I have to say, bully for her."

"My God, we are a catty pair. Let's simply accept that she's happy and be thrilled for her."

Brenda and Ann decided that Kim could determine the date and hopefully Ray would be home to do a BBQ. The weather was starting to warm up as March turned to April. Kim was delighted at the invitation and informed Ann that the forecast for Tuesday was to be unusually warm and dry. They agreed to cocktails at 6:00. As it happened, Ray was home that day so it looked like the evening was a go.

Kim and Boris arrived right on time and Ray met them and ushered them directly to the back yard. As Ray led them down the hallway, the conversation centred around the current virus situation and everyone agreed to try to keep some distance between each other to be on the safe side.

Ann rushed to meet Brenda when she arrived. "You are not going to believe this. Boris *is* tall, handsome, and charming! Not only that, he was educated in England so has almost no foreign accent. Kim is radiant."

Brenda and Ann moved to the back yard where Ann put the pastries Brenda had brought beside a bottle of wine that Boris had handed her when they arrived. Ray and Boris were chatting away.

Kim rushed to give Brenda a big hug, managing to present her diamond at the same time so Brenda could admire it.

And admire it she did.

Kim grabbed Brenda's hand and guided her across the lawn to introduce her to Boris.

Gentle breezes of warm spring air and the sweet smells of freshly mown grass wafted in the air, a pleasant reminder of spring weather. Ray had mowed that afternoon, the first of the year. The warm evening and good company lifted everyone's spirits. Ann soon went into the house to get a bulky black sweater. She wrapped her arms around herself trying to keep her body heat in.

"Are you okay, love?" Ray leaned over Ann with a concerned look on his face. "The rest of us are quite warm, yet you seem chilled."

"It's likely that low-blood thing. I should get the results of the tests this week. Nothing to worry about, a little shot of iron should set me right. The sooner the better."

As the evening drew to a close, everyone promised to get together on a regular basis.

Chapter 13

The news the following morning changed those plans. The Province did move forward to close down almost every site where people gathered. All Ann's seminars and signing engagements were cancelled. Social distancing was mandated, and life became a battle of restrictions.

Three days later, Ann received a call from Doctor Burns. The doctor's voice was professional and direct. "Ann, can you and Ray come in this afternoon for a consultation?"

"Why Ray?"

"It's always a good thing to have someone with you when there are details that need to be remembered. Ray can take notes as I discuss your symptoms."

Ann hung up the phone after having made an appointment for 11:00 the following morning. She approached Ray who was watching golf on TV.

"Can you mute that for a minute please?"

Ray pushed the button and was alarmed to see how disturbed Ann was when she told him about the doctor's call.

"Honey, I am scared. There must be more to this than a simple iron deficiency. I think we're looking at something serious and that's why she asked for you to come with me."

Ray jumped up and gathered Ann into his arms. "Medical advances have come so far that it's likely a condition that requires some simple surgery or something. Let's not get ahead of ourselves by worrying about what it is until we know what the diagnosis is."

Ann wrapped a blanket around her shoulders and reached for

her laptop. She Googled her symptoms and found a whole rash of possibilities. They went from easy-to-cure to severe options. Ann decided that Ray was right: they would have to wait until her appointment.

"Ann. Instead of sitting here worrying about what might be, why don't we go to Luigi's and pig out on good Italian food, then take in a movie?"

"Good thought. But, Ray. All the restaurants are closed. So are the theatres. We are locked down. I do have spaghetti sauce in the freezer. We can do our own version of Italian right here."

"Great. I'll check to see if there's a good movie on TV."

Ray headed for the den and Ann for the kitchen.

Ann assembled TV-style dinners and they got out the folding tables and decided to watch *Paradise Road*. Ann was wrapped in a blanket and after eating, leaned against Ray, taking in his warmth. Ray stroked her back then his hand wandered to her breast then to her stomach.

"Well that's one way of warming me up. We've seen this movie so many times, why don't we continue this petting in bed?"

"Ray grinned, stood up and picked Ann up, blanket and all.

"There's no way you are carrying me upstairs. Put me down, you big lug, before you injure yourself."

They laughed all the way to the bedroom.

*****

The next morning, Ann got out of bed at daybreak, tired from lack of sleep. She could not get rid of the feeling of dread. She brewed coffee and went to her computer to once again research her symptoms. Her doctor's appointment wasn't until late morning, so she had hours to worry about the possibilities. She tried to work on her novel, but could not concentrate. She ended up pacing the house from the kitchen, where she refilled her coffee cup, carrying it with her as she went to the living room windows. She stared out at the street, but was not registering anything she saw. All she could think about was what her diagnosis was going to be.

With her thoughts so far away, she hadn't heard Ray come up behind her.

He wrapped his arms around her and held her close. "No matter what we're faced with, we will get through it together. You complete me and I need you to make me whole. Honey, believe me, there's nothing we cannot overcome."

"But what if it's cancer?"

"There's no point in guessing. There's no point in looking at the worst scenario. It's likely low blood, like Elsie says. Let's try to busy ourselves. I for one want to take a look at the garden. Lots of perennials are poking through. Want to come with me?"

Ann was not up to running, so a walk around the garden was ideal. Ray and Ann both refilled their coffee cups and wandered outside. Planning their garden was always one of the things they shared and looked forward to every year.

"Since I'll likely be around more, I want to plant another perennial garden over there near the fence." Ray was pointing to the far end of the lot. "It gets lots of sunshine and the soil can be enriched with compost and nutrients. What do you think?"

"Great idea. Can we plant delphiniums and larkspur?"

"Make a list of anything you think of, and I'll think about placement and decide what might work." Ray reached for Ann's hand, noting how cold it was. "Are you feeling chilled?"

"Yes, I think I'll go inside and warm up."

Ray watched her and a frown of concern furrowed his brow. He clenched his stomach muscles to contain the dreaded fear that raced through his thoughts. He married late in life, never having found the perfect mate until he met Ann. She was twenty years younger than he was but that was never a problem. When they started dating, her father was somewhat reluctant to welcome him into the family as Stan and Ray were almost the same age. Yet over the years, they became close friends as well as in-laws. Stan finally admitted that Ann was an old soul in a young body, so Ray was the perfect mate. Once Elsie and Stan realized that Ray and Ann were meant for each other, they accepted the match.

Now, Ray was faced with wondering how ill Ann was and what lay in the future. Surely the doctor would alleviate his fears when they went for the appointment later in the morning.

The parking lot at the clinic was full and Ray had to drive around several times before a spot became vacant. He backed in between a white cargo van and a red sports car. As they walked to the entrance, Ray held firmly to Ann's hand, squeezing it now and again just to confirm he was there to support her.

Contrary to their mood, the morning sun beamed down making fog from the previous night's rain hover over the tarmac. Ray held the door open for an elderly couple to exit before he and Ann entered. The receptionist handed them each a mask and directed them to the waiting area, saying they would be seen shortly.

As Ann often did, she started to fuss with Ray's outfit. She smoothed his blue plaid shirt collar, tucked in a loose bit above his beige cords. Ray took her hand and gave her a decisive do-not-touch look. They quickly sat to avoid the attention and noticed the chairs were staggered about six feet apart. Ray moved one so they could be close together. They were barely seated when they were called and ushered into a small examination room. Ann and Ray sat in the utilitarian chairs with their black faux-leather seats, while they waited for Doctor Burns. There were charts and information on the bland, beige walls. Ray started to read them out loud.

"Ulcers are caused by …"

The doctor came into the office with a big smile and greeted them. She reached for Ann's hand then Ray's and shook each with a strong, yet gentle hold. She pulled her chair forward when she sat down on it and reached for her keyboard and scrolled through her computer until the screen was where she wanted. She took a moment to read what was there.

"Ann, we received the results of your blood tests and the second set was consistent with the first. There is strong evidence that this is a possible blood-related condition."

"See? Elsie's right. It's simply a matter of boosting your iron." Ray was all smiles.

"I wish that was all we were dealing with. I'm afraid it's more complex than that. Your white cell count is far too high. Now this is not definite, but there's a strong possibility we are dealing with a form of leukemia. One that I want either confirmed or ruled out."

"What?" Both Ann and Ray interjected.

"At this point, I want you to see an oncologist at the cancer clinic at the General Hospital. I took the liberty to book an appointment for Friday. I know this is Wednesday so you will not have a lot of time to think about what you might be facing. Don't be alarmed. There have been a lot of positive strides in medicine to treat leukemia, and Doctor Helms is one of the best physicians in that field."

Ray leaned over toward the doctor. "So you are fairly convinced that Ann does have leukemia."

"All the symptoms and tests seem to point in that direction, yes. I do think this is what we are dealing with. I'm sorry, but I'd rather be honest. If Doctor Helms confirms my diagnosis, he will start treatment immediately. We do not want to postpone getting started."

Ann sat in stunned silence.

"What will the treatment be?" Ray stroked Ann's hand.

"I will let Doctor Helms outline that for you. He's the expert. And based on the tests, and what we know about your medical history, he will determine what steps to take. Try not to think the worst. As I said, great strides have been made in this field. Doctor Helms will keep me informed of your progress. I wish I had better news for you, but on the up side, Ann, you take good care of yourself. You contacted me early. That is a good thing. The sooner treatment is started, the better. The medical professionals are currently dealing with this Covid-19 virus so have postponed a lot of patients' appointments. However, your case will not be impacted. You will get the best of care right away."

Ray and Ann left the clinic with a heavy silence hovering over them. When they got into the car, Ray leaned over and kissed Ann's cheek. "Okay, that was a bit of a surprise. I was scheduled to fly on Friday but there's no way I'm letting you go to the cancer clinic alone. I'll request a leave until we know what you'll — No. What *we'll* be facing. I'll reschedule my flights to always be there for you. Since most passenger flights have been cancelled or postponed, this pandemic issue works in our favour."

"I just can't assimilate this. It doesn't make sense. My diet's healthy. I exercise. I take extremely good care of myself. How could I be diagnosed with cancer? That's what it is, isn't it? A form of cancer? Before my appointment, I want to research everything I can."

"We will look together. I, for one, want to see the latest strides the medical field have taken and get an idea what you and I will be facing."

Ann's Friday appointment was booked for 8:00 in the morning which meant they had to leave early, due to rush-hour traffic.

"It's a good thing we allowed extra time, the cars are crawling. Simply stop and go." Ann watched the lanes of vehicles barely moving. "Frankly, this suits my mood. I would rather never get there but of course, I know I must. Ray. I'm so scared. Everything we found on line did nothing to allay my fears."

"Me too. I'm glad we did all that research because I think I will understand what the doctor is telling us. Relax. We'll still get there on time even though the traffic is dead slow." Ray noticed how Ann was wringing her hands and zipping and unzipping her purse.

Once they were past the intersection of Prince of Wales and Hunt Club, they turned onto Riverside Drive where the cars were moving at a better pace. Within minutes, they were at the entrance to the General Hospital. Ray followed the signs to The Cancer Clinic entrance at the back and had no problem finding a parking space. A light rain was starting so they hustled across the tarmac and through the doorway. They walked along the hallway until they approached a lady at a desk. The receptionist directed them to the right area and notified Dr. Helms's assistant that they had arrived. They walked along the hall to the farthest area, marked C, and were about to be seated when Ann's name was called.

They were led to a sparsely furnished office that had only a few diplomas on the wall. Ray was quick to find Dr. Helms's, and let out a low whistle. "This guy has more letters behind his name than Einstein."

A soft laugh preceded a tall, lean man in a white lab coat as he stepped through the door. He had obviously heard Ray. His tanned complexion revealed that he spent a lot of time outdoors. He appeared to be athletic, and much younger than either Ray or Ann thought he would be.

Dr. Helms shook their hands before easing his long frame into the office-style chair and rolled and swiveled to face them.

"I have gone over the files Doctor Burns sent. I understand that she told you she suspected that it was a form of leukemia. I have to say, I agree. I'm sure you were hoping to hear otherwise, but all the tests and symptoms point in that direction. In order to confirm this diagnosis, I want to admit you to the hospital and do a complete series of tests."

Ann leaned forward with fists clenched to prevent herself from bursting onto tears. "When would you like me to be admitted?"

"Actually, it would be good if you could stay right now. Or after I explain everything. First, we need to assess your general health outside of this issue. This will involve checking your vital signs to see if you have a fever, shortness of breath or rapid heartbeat. We will do an overall examination to check your skin for bruising and paleness, feel areas of the neck, underarm and groin for any swollen, or enlarged, lymph nodes. We will also check your mouth for infections, bleeding or swollen gums, check your abdomen for enlarged organs and examine your skeleton for tenderness or pain. I have a team waiting to get started. The lab will do a more-complete blood check to measure the number and quality of white blood cells, red blood cells and platelets. Leukemia causes abnormal blood cell counts. That's how Doctor Burns came to the conclusion she did. Your blood cell counts were quite abnormal.

"Just so you are aware, there are other conditions that cause abnormal blood cell counts. Leukemia cells are not normally seen in the blood, so doctors will suspect leukemia if there are blasts or blood cells that do not look normal. We need to rule out all other possibilities.

"Levels of some chemicals may be higher than normal with leukemia. They, too, can be determined by blood tests. I want to do the tests over the next two days. The sooner I know what we're dealing with, the sooner we can start treatment. There's one thing, though. Should the tests indicate leukemia, I would like to do a lumbar puncture — a spinal tap — to remove a small amount of cerebrospinal fluid from the space around the spine to look at it under a microscope. A lumbar puncture is done to see if cancer has spread to the spinal fluid. All this might sound frightening at this time, but you were diagnosed early, which is a good thing. I want to rule out every possible reason you are experiencing the problems you are."

Ray stroked the back of Ann's hand. "How soon will we know the results of all those tests?"

"Almost immediately. Depending on the results, I may consult other physicians that specialize in this area, too. I always feel the more input the better. If it's okay with you, Ann, my nurse will help you with the paperwork and get you settled in."

Ann and Ray both nodded.

A nurse dressed in a flowery pink blouse and matching pants arrived on cue and indicated with a wide smile that they should follow her. Without a word, Ann stood, patted her black skirt down to get rid of the wrinkles from sitting, and followed this large friendly woman along the hallway.

Ray quickly joined her. In less than a half hour, they were being ushered to a ward and Ann was issued a hospital gown.

"I'm sorry, Mr. Rogers, but you have to leave now." The nurse's tone was firm yet calming.

Ray turned to leave, then over his shoulder told Ann that he would return with items she would need.

"I'll call you later and tell you what to bring. Love you."

"Love you back." Ray navigated the hallways unaware of what was happening around him. The need to get to the car then home before he burst into tears was all he could think about. Everything seemed surreal.

Chapter 14

When Ray got home, he poured a stiff drink of scotch, drank it neat, and let it warm his body. Lunch was not an option; he was nauseous and felt confused. He debated whether to call Elsie, then decided that Ann needed to be consulted first. He roamed the house from room to room, made coffee then let it sit and go cold. He stepped out to the back deck, looked up at the sky and yelled at the top of his lungs. "Why? Why Ann?"

"Why are you shouting?" Stan had entered the house quietly and had followed Ray out to the deck. When Ray turned around, his face was streaked with tears.

"God, Stan. I don't know how to say this. Come into the kitchen and I'll pour us each a glass."

Stan, with a look of concern, went to the kitchen and took down another glass from the cupboard while Ray went to the liquor cabinet. He didn't question Ray. He waited for what he would be told. Stan steeled for the worst because he knew Ray seldom drank in the middle of the day. He took off his Adirondack jacket and pushed up the sleeves of his cable-knit Aran sweater, and waited to hear what Ray had to say.

"I really came by to drop off some cranberry muffins that Elsie baked this morning."

It was obvious that Ray was not interested in muffins, so Stan set the glasses on the counter and waited. Ray poured a generous serving, lifted the glasses, and handed the fresh one to Stan at the same time indicating that they move to the den.

"I left Ann at the hospital. She'll be undergoing extensive tests today and tomorrow."

Stan set his glass on the coffee table. "What do you mean? What's wrong?" Stan had stopped in the middle of lowering himself to a burgundy leather recliner. He stood back up and stared at Ray.

Ray took a mouthful of the amber liquid, swallowed it then cleared his throat. "I wasn't going to tell you until we knew for sure, and I wanted Ann to be with me, but since you're here, I could use some support. It's quite possible that Ann has leukemia."

"What! No. That's impossible! She's always taken such good care of herself. Proper diet, lots of exercise ... And she's adamant that a good night's sleep is important. There must be some mistake." This time Stan dropped into the chair.

"Doctor Burns ran two sets of bloodwork and referred her to an oncologist. He tentatively agrees with Doctor Burns. The new tests will rule out any other possibilities. We simply have to wait and see. God, Stan. I'm so scared."

The two men sat staring at the wall noting nothing in particular. The silence weighed heavy, the air was oppressive.

Stan turned and raised his bushy eyebrows and looked off to a place beyond the window. "I'll have to tell Elsie. She will not handle this well."

"No. Wait until we know for sure and until Ann asks me to tell her mother. Honestly, Stan, I'm not sure what I'll do if the tests confirm leukemia. Ann's my sole reason for being. I can't lose her." Tears welled up in Ray's eyes and he turned his back on Stan as he blew his nose and composed himself. "We should know tomorrow or the next day. I'll keep you posted. Ann has to stay in hospital so extensive testing can be done."

Stan stepped forward and placed his hands on Ray's

shoulders. "We'll get through this together. Have you told Brenda yet?"

"No. Again, we'll wait until we have the final results."

Stan pulled a large handkerchief out of his back pocket and wiped his cheeks that were wet from tears then blew his nose with a large snort. He reached for the phone that was ringing at his right shoulder and handed it to Ray.

"Hello. Yes, this is he."

The tense expression on Ray's face led Stan to believe it might be the doctor.

Ray turned to hang up the phone. "It was Ann's doctor. He wants me to be with her as soon as I can. Apparently, some test results are already in today. This does not sound good. I'll call you later."

Ray saw Stan to the front door, picked up his keys from the hall table, and locked up the house.

Both men stood facing each other before leaving, nodded, then left in their cars.

Ray drove slowly and carefully as his heart was racing and his vision kept blurring with threatening tears.

Ann sent Ray a text saying she would meet him in the waiting area outside the doctor's office.

She was waiting when he arrived. Ray wrapped her in his arms. "Well you smell more like a hospital than your usual flowery soap."

Ann laughed at the intent to lighten the moment. She was fully dressed in her slacks and sweater but carried her raincoat.

They were called by a nurse and ushered into an office and sat in chairs in front of the desk.

Doctor Helms came in as they were seated and he closed the

door behind him before he crossed the floor to his chair. His sandy hair flopped over his forehead belying the solemn expression on his face. Brushing his hand across his brow to push the hair back, he leaned forward. "I wish I had good news for you, but all the tests confirm what we had feared. That being said, because, Ann, you have taken such good care of yourself, there is definitely promising expectations that treatment will be successful. We were going to keep you here tonight, but the tests were so conclusive, you might as well be at home."

Trembling, Ann asked what was going to happen next.

"There are a lot of things that come into play here. First, we had to consider your age, your general health or fitness and any other illnesses you have. In your case, it's all good. That being said, I want to begin aggressive treatment right away. In the past few weeks, there have been considerable changes happening to the genes and chromosomes of your CLL cells."

He noted a puzzled expression on both Ann's and Ray's faces.

"Since the word 'cancer' is not in the name, many people do not know that lymphoma is a type of cancer. Signs and symptoms of this little-understood disease often go unnoticed and are even undetected by healthcare professionals. This cancer can be overwhelming and devastating for patients and their families. CLL or chronic lymphocytic leukemia is a type of blood cancer. In people with CLL, the body makes too many abnormal lymphocytes. These abnormal lymphocytes look normal under a microscope, but they do not fight infections like healthy lymphocytes do. Although it is called leukemia, CLL is actually a type of blood cancer called lymphoma. Thinking of CLL as a lymphoma is important, because CLL behaves and is treated like other slow-growing lymphomas.

"Over two thousand people in Canada are diagnosed with CLL each year. CLL is more common in men and occurs mainly in people over sixty. You, Ann, are the exception. When most of the cancer cells are in the blood stream and the bone marrow, it is called CLL. When the cancer cells are mostly found in the lymph nodes, it is called SLL. In your case, CLL. CLL usually progresses slowly. In many cases, it causes few, if any, problems in its early stages. Many people have CLL that is slow growing and they may have stable disease for years with few or no symptoms. Other people with CLL have a faster-growing form of the disease that may cause more symptoms and need treatment sooner. I believe this is what we are dealing with."

"This is very frightening. How do I deal with dying?"

"Because your family physician diagnosed your symptoms early, I firmly believe that treatment will be successful. We need to begin with aggressive chemo to attack the blood cells. That being said, in conjunction with chemo, I would like to move right to a bone marrow transplant. Bone marrow, the soft, spongy tissue inside the large bones in the body, can be affected by a variety of blood disorders, blood cancers and other diseases." The doctor rolled his chair closer to Ann and picked up her hands.

"I know this is frightening but you need to understand both the medical explanation and what you will be facing. Hematopoietic stem cells live in the bone marrow and give rise to all of the other components of the blood. Bone marrow makes red blood cells which carry oxygen to all the tissues in the body. White blood cells fight infection. I know this may sound overwhelming, but it will all make more sense as we move forward. As soon as we can find a bone marrow donor, the sooner we can defeat this invasion to your body."

"Where would I find a donor?"

"Preferably a family member. A sibling is often the best match."

"I'm an only child. What about my mother or father?"

"We'll do an analysis to see if there's a match. Any relative might be the right diagnostic fit. We'll go into further detail about this in the coming days. I think you have enough to absorb right now."

"I fear telling my parents. Since I'm their only child, they'll be devastated."

"Let me give you some pointers. Make the first move by telling them about your lymphoma. Do not emphasize the word 'cancer', as commonly, people are terrified of that term. Many people do not really understand leukemia, so give them information in small chunks. And check to make sure they understand. Be as honest as possible about your own feelings. They need to know if you are frightened, and they may feel the same emotions that you are feeling. Share with them. Let them know what to expect during your treatment, and how they can help. Be prepared for difficult questions and answer them honestly. Often, the greatest fears come from not knowing."

"Her mother will have a hard time with this but I already told her father so he'll be prepared for the news."

"I'm glad you have family that'll be supportive. Ann, I will schedule chemo to start on Monday. In the meantime, learn as much as you possibly can about what you will undergo in the next few months. Don't hesitate to phone my office if anything is bothering you. Never feel that your concerns are too trite to call. All questions are important."

Doctor Helms stood up and reached for several pamphlets, which he handed to Ann. "You will be contacted, probably later today, with what time to come in for treatment."

Ray reached for the doctor's hand, shook it, then helped Ann stand. She was visibly shaken. She thanked Doctor Helms and followed Ray out of the office.

Once in the car, Ann dissolved into tears. Ray held her until she regained some control. "Okay, Fly Boy. You are going to have to kick me if I keep feeling sorry for myself. I need to be strong and beat this bloody thing. Well now. That expression fits." A weak smile spread across her face.

Ray leaned over to give her a hand a firm squeeze and a gentle kiss on the forehead.

"Well my dear? I really don't want to be passionate in a hospital parking lot. What say we head home, pour a glass of wine and have sex?"

Ann burst out laughing. "Trust a male to cure all ills with sex!"

Chapter 15

Ann wakened in the night dripping wet and tense with fear. *This diagnosis has stripped me bare, peeled away all my strengths and my inner self is screaming. I don't know who I am or how I will find the way to deal with facing invasive treatments.*

She let out a cry from deep within that startled Ray awake. He reached for Ann and drew her close. "You frightened me. That noise did not even sound like you, rather ghoulish and pained."

" Oh, Ray. I'm so frightened. This whole thing has unnerved me and left me mentally bruised and raw."

"We *will* get through this together. You're a strong person and you need to draw on that strength to get through the months to come. Once we've told your mother, Brenda and other close friends, you'll have a strong support group. I've decided to take a year's leave of absence to be here for you."

"No, Ray. Don't. Take a few weeks. I'd appreciate that as I'll need you, but you will go crazy hanging around for a full year. Let's take it week by week. I dread telling Elsie and Brenda but know it must be done."

"You're shaking. Are you cold?"

Ann snuggled closer to Ray. "Yes."

Ray rubbed Ann's back and kissed her forehead. "Try to go back to sleep. You need all the rest you can get."

Ann got up early and was showered and dressed before Ray opened his eyes. "I smell coffee." Ray yawned and stretched.

"Couldn't sleep any longer. Thought I would try to concentrate on the next chapter in the book. You go back to sleep. I'm fine."

With a wave, Ann left the bedroom and went to the kitchen where she poured a cup of coffee that she carried to her office. She had spent months painting and decorating, making her office a place where she would be creative yet relaxed. One wall was hung with covers of her novels and a few framed awards. This soft buttercup-yellow background blended into the deep sand of the other walls. Over her desk, a large landscape of waves breaking on a sandy shore dominated. Three small, still-life drawings of varied flowers, beautifully executed, drew one's admiration. Dawn was breaking and Ann stood for a few moments at the window, watching the sky turn from a bright-yellow glow to daylight. A few clouds were scattered here and there, but the day looked promising. Ann opened the window a crack to let the sweet smells of spring in. She fired up her computer and was soon lost in the characters' happenings of her story.

Two hours later, Ray peeked into Ann's office with a questioning look on his face.

"This has been more therapeutic than I could have imagined. For some reason, my main character blossomed and became the person I have been striving to write for months." Ann closed her laptop, stood, stretched her weary back and followed Ray into the kitchen.

"I know you're in a better frame of mind than yesterday, but we have to deal with your mother. Stan knows and we need to tell Elsie before he blabs."

"You told Stan?"

"I told you at the doctor's office. I guess you didn't hear me. It was kind of a male bonding thing. Stan came by while you were in the hospital. I needed support and Stan was there for me."

"Well that explains it. I'm glad he was there for you." Ann

pulled her phone out of her pocket and dialed her mother. "Are you decent? Ray and I want to come over for a few minutes. There's something we want to discuss with you."

"Sure, honey. No problem. Your dad and I were reading the newspaper and getting ourselves ready to go shopping."

"We'll be over shortly." Ann sagged against the counter. "Lord, Ray. I really don't want to go but know I must."

"You'll do fine. It's Elsie who will fall apart, so you need to be my Iron Gal."

***

Stan knew by the look on Ray's face as soon as he saw him that the news was not good. He immediately moved to be beside Elsie who was sitting at the kitchen table. She had set out freshly baked banana bread and butter.

The smells of freshly brewed coffee enticed Ray and Ann to fill a mug each before they took a seat. Ann reached over, took her mother's hand in hers and told Elsie her news.

"There must be some mistake, Ann. You are healthy and keep in shape. No. It must be an error. Doctors can make mistakes, you know. I'm sure it's just low iron."

Stan placed his hands on Elsie's shoulders. "The tests are conclusive. There is *no* mistake."

Elsie looked deep into Ann's eyes, stunned by the news. Trembling, she clutched Ann's hand tight. She drew in a sharp sigh. "My darling girl, this is the most devastating news. I knew you were feeling chilled and sometimes a little dizzy, but I can't even begin to consider it was something so serious. Oh my God, how will we solve this calamity?"

"That's a strange way to put it but I'll start chemo on Monday.

Since the bone marrow is affected, the doctor has suggested that a bone marrow transplant might be required."

"What does that mean?"

Simply put, it means removing the diseased cells and replacing them with healthy ones from a qualified donor. It's a relatively simple surgical procedure."

"How do they determine who can be a donor?"

"The first step is to ask family members if they are willing to donate cells, and then tests are undertaken to determine if they're a match for the patient. Siblings are much more likely to be matches than parents, but only about thirty percent of people needing a transplant will have a compatibly matched sibling."

"How do we take the test?"

"Actually, it's very easy. The prospective donor provides a cheek swab sample, and this is used to compare specific genetic markers, known as human leukocyte antigens, HLA. These markers determine if the donor matches the patient in need of a bone marrow transplant."

"If we match, what next?"

"You will be contacted to confirm that you are willing to donate. Then you will undergo further blood tests and physical exams to ensure that the donation is safe for both of us. Once everything is confirmed as medically eligible, both the patient and donor undergo pre-transplant treatments to prepare their bodies for the transplant."

"How soon can we check to see if we qualify?" Stan had moved into the only vacant chair and was leaning forward to catch her every word.

"The doctor indicated that he could make arrangements quickly."

"So if we are suitable, what next?"

"Bone marrow donation is a short, surgical procedure performed under anesthesia. The surgical team inserts hollow needles and withdraws stem cells from the bone marrow at the back of the pelvic bones of the donor."

Elsie screwed up her face. "It sounds awful. Is there a recovery time for the donor?"

"There are a few common side effects after marrow donation. The donor might experience lower back pain or discomfort, fatigue, throat pain, muscle pain and insomnia. However, most donors recover well and are back to their normal routine within several days. During transplant, the donor's healthy blood-forming cells are transfused into the patient's bloodstream and settle in the bone marrow where they begin manufacturing new blood-forming cells. It can take several days to find out if the transplant was successful."

"You have to tell Brenda and Jason. I'm sure they'll want to try to be donors, too." Stan was trailing his hands through his hair; his bushy eyebrows were raised in alarm. "I hate needles but I'll go through anything to make my precious daughter healthy again."

Elsie looked at Stan then stood up and walked away.

"Where's Mom going?"

"I expect she just needs to think. This is a bit of a blockbuster. Thanks to Ray, I had some time to think about it and did do some research."

"I appreciate that you kept it to yourself. I wanted to be the one to tell her. God, Dad. It's such a rotten thing to be faced with. Ray's been great and I keep falling apart but he's definitely my strength. Please help Mom. Both Ray and I will need you every step of the way. Now, Ray and I are going over to Brenda's. She'll go ape on me."

Ray and Stan chuckled at Ann's choice of words.

Since it was Sunday, Brenda would be home.

Ray drove. Ann lowered the window to breathe in the fresh smells of spring. She watched robins scurrying around lawns and saw Canada geese formations clutter the sky. When they got to Brenda's, the car was not there. No one was home. Ann pulled out her cell phone and dialed Brenda to ask where she was.

"Hi, Ann. I'm on my way home. I just picked up Dan. He's a grump so watch out."

Ann laughed. "Typical teenager. They can turn on a moment. When you get home, I want to have a serious talk. And Dan should be a part of the conversation."

***

Ray and Ann had let themselves in with their own set of keys. When Brenda and Dan arrived, they were sitting at the kitchen table nursing glasses of red wine.

Ray stood up and got a glass for Brenda while Dan poured himself a large glass of milk.

Brenda had a querying expression on her face, knowing that wine so early in the day was unusual. The words came easier now as Ann told her extended family what was going on with her body.

Brenda's reaction was immediate. She jumped up and pounded the wall, stamped her feet and burst into tears then crumpled into Ray's waiting arms.

"I can't lose my best friend. I can't."

Ray handed her a tissue and told her to calm down.

"We won't lose Ann. We'll fight this with everything we can.

She has the most-qualified oncologist in his field and Ottawa has one of the finest clinics."

After Brenda settled down, she was filled in on all the procedures and told what was ahead. Immediately, she, too, asked to be a donor. Dan sat in his chair without saying a word.

After his mother had offered to donate, he nodded his head. "Me too. Can I donate?" His grumpy mood had dissolved.

"I think so. You have no idea how blessed I am to have such wonderful friends. Knowing that you are here for me gives me strength to bear all of the treatment I'll be facing. Even the chemo crap."

"Well. I presume you're going to be off alcohol for the time being. I suggest we get roaring drunk!" Brenda opened the cupboard and took out another bottle of wine. Dan excused himself saying he needed to talk to Li.

"Yep. Getting roaring drunk sounds like a plan." Ann had a grin on her face.

Brenda raised her glass. "Never hesitate to drink to my dearest friend's health. Here's to being leukemia free." She downed her wine and refilled her glass.

"Here's to chemo and bone marrow transplants. May they work their magic."

Ann smiled at her friend's reaction to what was to come. She knew that Brenda would be there for her every step of the way. It was reassuring. Sitting there drinking her wine, she felt stronger, and the will to fight flared up. "I will shiver, puke and hate the treatment but I will endure." Ann raised her glass high. "I only hope it doesn't take long to finish the treatments because I'm looking forward to my next glass of wine."

Chapter 16

The text came later that evening to be at the hospital early in the morning and be prepared to be there for the entire morning. Ray drove Ann to the hospital and left her with the clinician.

The technician helping Ann in the cancer clinic explained the process, "Chemotherapy, a combination of drugs, is used to destroy as many leukemia cells as possible and bring blood counts to normal. We start with lesser intensified doses then increase them as we see how you tolerate them. Continued intensification chemotherapy is intended to destroy remaining leukemia cells that cannot be seen in the blood or bone marrow. While chemotherapy destroys rapidly dividing cancer cells, it may also affect normal fast-growing cells, such as those in the hair, mouth and bone marrow. Chemotherapy for leukemia may also temporarily interfere with the ability of the bone marrow to produce adequate numbers of blood cells. Depending on the drugs used and your individual response, you may experience side effects. We are here to help you adjust to any adverse reaction. Most people have two rounds of induction chemotherapy. The treatment will be done here at the hospital as you'll need very close medical and nursing supervision. You'll probably be able to go home shortly after each treatment."

Ann sat there trying to absorb this information as she watched a drip being inserted into her left arm. She knew the treatment could take several hours and had brought her laptop to help pass the time.

The treatment area was bright and cheerful with muted

colours of lilac and yellow. Ann noted pots of blooming tulips and violets. She smiled at the technician and watched the slow drip of chemicals ease into her body. Thinking she would be able to write on her novel did not happen, as once she relaxed, she dozed off. The time passed quickly and Ray picked her up within minutes of the session ending.

"How's my favourite gal?"

"Starving! Can we stop at Bigger Burger and pig out?"

"Sure. I'm hungry too." Ray tapped the right-turn signal and headed along Riverside Drive. There was plenty of parking and he pulled into a spot beside a spotless, shining 4X4 RAM, right at the front entrance to the diner. As Ann stepped down, she grabbed the door handle and leaned back against the car.

"Ann! You okay?"

"Oh, one of those stupid dizzy spells. It's passed now. I guess I'll have to be careful not to stand up too quickly." She eased away from their maroon Corolla.

Ray reached over to swipe dirt from the car off her brown jacket.

They were stopped before entering to be informed that there was only curb-side service.

"This damn pandemic is changing our lives. Okay, let's order take-away. Both ordered up the Bigger Burger special and drove to Mooney's Bay to eat by the river.

"I'm not so starved now." Ann patted her stomach and laughed at how much they had eaten. "You know, I don't think either of us has finished a meal since my diagnosis. We were ready for this."

Nodding his head, Ray followed Ann to the car. Ann was telling him about what had happened at the clinic when her phone buzzed. She saw it was Elsie. Knowing she would be worried, Ann answered in her most cheerful voice.

"Oh, sweetheart. You sound great. How was it? Your father and I have been so worried."

"Ray and I went to Bigger Burger and each of us finished off the house special. I'm stuffed!"

"Are you going to drop by?"

"We promised Brenda that she could come by after work. Dan and Li are taking in a movie. I think she really just wanted to see that I'm still living and breathing. I feel fine. If this is what I have to go through, it will be a cinch."

When Brenda arrived, she rushed over and gave Ann a big hug. "We had a bonanza day at the yard so I am ready to drink wine and hear all about what my dearest friend went through today. By the way, Jorge is proving to be a godsend. He learns quickly and carries out his chores to the letter. Randy is thrilled with him. I have to submit his first report this coming week."

Brenda sank into the sofa beside Ann, grabbed her hand and stroked it. Ann had set up appointments for her potential donors for the following week. She told Brenda when hers was.

Ray left for the kitchen and returned with two glasses of wine, and lemonade for Ann. He left again and brought a platter of nibbling food. After the burgers, they were not hungry, but knew Brenda would be.

About two hours later, Ann announced that she was exhausted, so Brenda said her goodnights and left. Ann went to bed and Ray turned on the hockey game in the den.

The game was tense and Ray was totally engrossed in it when he heard Ann race to the bathroom. Concerned, he went to see if she was all right. He found her bent over the toilet retching and retching. He grabbed a face cloth, dampened it with cold water and wiped her forehead.

"Well that happened quickly! So much for burgers." Ann sat on the tile floor until she felt strong enough to stand. She wiped her face and gave Ray a weak smile as she leaned against him.

Ray held her elbow and walked her to the bed.

"Probably a good idea to put a sick-bucket by the bed. Can you get the down comforter for me, I'm freezing."

Over the next three days, Ann had ups and downs. She was not able to keep her food down, so ate small amounts often. Jason and Kim had both phoned. Jason expressed his concern and asked if Ann needed anything. She told each when they were scheduled to be swabbed for the bone marrow transplant. The doctor told her not to be disappointed if her family and friends did not produce a match as there was a donor bank and he would have his staff start a search in any event. Ann's family and friends were tested by Thursday, but results were discouraging as none qualified.

Once Jason learned that Ray had taken time off work, he suggested that Ann might like to take short walks instead of running the trails.

"That's a great idea. Are you sure you don't mind going with me? I would really like that. I don't want to go by myself. Your company would be a fantastic change to being with Ray all the time. Besides, he can use the time to run around and do chores. He's being a nuisance because he frets and will not let me be alone. That's not a complaint, just a fact. I do have to admit, though, that he is also a godsend. It's been four days since the chemo, and I feel I need to get out — to inhale fresh air. Can we go this afternoon?"

"Lace up, my friend. I will be over at two-thirty."

Jason arrived wearing a big smile and his jogging clothes. Ann always got a chuckle out of the fact that he wore red slim pants and a pink shirt with the LGBTQ rainbow printed on it. Jason was never afraid to put the word out.

"My dear, you look ravishing."

"Well I puked up all the bad stuff so only good remains." Ann wrapped her arms around Jason. "Due to this virus thingy, we are being advised to form a bubble group of only ten people. You, Mom, Dad, Ray, Brenda, and Dan are in mine."

"That works as Warren and I have decided to cut most activities."

"Also, the chemotherapy reduces my immune system, so I have to be extra careful. Now that spring is here, I hope the distancing issues disappear soon."

"Outside of you and Warren, my social group is small. I will insist that everyone else will have to keep six feet away and wear a mask."

"Okay. Off we go."

Jason and Ann walked along the trail with the understanding that if Ann started to tire, they would turn around. The fresh air was rejuvenating and Ann picked up her stride. As they were crossing an open field, Ann thought she heard a noise like a child crying. She stopped to listen.

"Are you okay? Do you need to turn around?" Jason eased up beside Ann.

"No. I thought I heard something. Did you?"

"Just my own breathing. I love being out in this field where the noisy cars don't pollute the sound this far away." Jason was running in place.

"I guess I imagined it. I would like to continue for another fifteen minutes before we turn around."

Ann set off at a faster pace. She quickly realized that she couldn't keep it up and slowed to a slow walk. "Let's go back."

Jason watched Ann with a concerned look on his face. "Sure hope you can make it. I'm not up to carrying you."

Ann chuckled and assured him she was fine and was pleased to get the exercise. When they were nearly back to the spot where Ann had thought she heard a noise, she stopped, grabbed Jason's arm and put her finger to her lips indicating he should be quiet.

At that moment, both she and Jason heard a soft cry. They exchanged querying looks. Jason edged closer to the sound, stopped and beckoned Ann over. Lying in the grass was a tiny kitten. Jason gathered it up and handed it to Ann.

"Oh, you little sweetheart. Why are you here all alone? Jason. Its fur is all matted and I can feel its ribs. It's starving. We can't leave it here."

"Honey, I can't take it home. Warren is dreadfully allergic. You will have to take care of it. In case it belongs to someone and has escaped, you need to post it on Facebook."

Ann wrapped the wee kitten in her shirt and took it home. She found a good-sized box in the garage and lined it with an old towel. Before she put the kitten into the box, she washed the excrement off its backside and gave it a saucer of milk which it lapped up immediately. No sooner had she set it on the towel than it pushed its wee face into a fold and went to sleep.

"Hey, little guy. You know you've found a safe place."

Ann went directly to her computer and posted a notice of Found Kitten. There was no response that afternoon. When Ray came home, he saw the kitten in the box, scooped it up and sought Ann. She explained.

"I hope nobody claims it. I love it already." The kitten had snuggled into his neck and was purring loudly.

"For a wee thing, she has a good set of pipes!"

"He or she?" Ray turned the kitten over and determined that it was a boy. "What will we call him?"

"Ray, don't get attached. I posted a query on Facebook and he might belong to someone."

"I know, but Snuggles is likely staying." Ray set off to check Google to see what to feed a kitten and how to care for one. Ann leaned against the wall and watched her tall, athletic husband completely captivated by a small furry creature.

"I'm exhausted. I need to have a rest. You're in charge of the baby."

Ray grinned and stroked the bundle purring next to his left ear.

After three days, no one had responded to the Facebook posting so Ann and Ray mutually agreed that it had found a new home. Ray cut away the front of the box so Snuggles could get in and out easily. A litter box was set close by and Snuggles soon figured out the house routine and settled right in. He did not like to be alone, though, so seldom used the sleeping box. He followed Ann or Ray wherever they went. He was fastidious about using the litter. They set him in the box with cuddly blankets at night but would wake in the morning to find Snuggles nestled in their bed, usually at the top of one of the pillows. Once Snuggles knew someone was awake, he purred loudly.

"This little fellow has stolen our hearts." Ann bent to ruffle Snuggles's coat and give a small tug to his tail. Snuggles leaned against her leg in appreciation.

Ray and Ann took him to an animal care centre the following

week and learned that the kitten was still very young and should not have been away from its mother. The veterinarian was surprised it had survived. Ann and Ray left with a kitten formula and special foods. They also made an appointment for Snuggles's first vaccination. From the vet's they went to the pet store to buy a carrying case, a brush and proper dishes.

Ray was standing in front of a display in an aisle. "He needs a toy. What do you think about this ball with a bell inside?"

"Perfect. I think this little mousy thingy is so cute." Ann added it to the cart. Before they left, Snuggles had five new toys, a crate, a bowl for water and one for food and a huge soft pillow. "Well he didn't like the box anyway."

On the way home, Ann realized she had not returned a voicemail message from Kim. She pulled out her cell and called. Kim wanted to know how Ann was doing and if she was well enough to visit the farm. She had a new foal that she was anxious to show Ann. They set a date for the next day.

"I need to get lots of rest, but I don't have another treatment until the day after tomorrow so, yes, we would love to come for a short visit tomorrow. Due to the treatment my immune system is weakened so I must practise social distancing and wear a mask. I'd appreciate it if you did likewise."

"Great idea! Snuggles can travel in his new carrying case."

"Ray, are you nuts?' You don't take a cat on outings."

"Why not? He won't be happy being left at home."

After a little back and forth, it was determined that Snuggles would be left at home, closed in with his litter box set beside the washing machine, and his new pillow, food and a cuddly teddy bear across from it.

Chapter 17

Ray followed the directions to Kim's farm. They had never been there before and were not very familiar with the east end of the city, let alone the countryside. Kin said her ranch backed onto Mer Bleue. Mer Bleue Bog was a protected area east of Ottawa. Its main feature was a sphagnum bog that was situated in an ancient channel of the Ottawa River. It was a remarkable boreal-like ecosystem normally not found that far south.

Once they were past the city and approaching Navan, Ann spotted a turnoff that had a typical, ranch-style entrance announced by a sign that stretched across the lane, attached to two tall elm trees. Tall Tree Ranch was aptly named.

"This is impressive. I wonder when Kim bought this place." Ray eased the car along slowly so they could take in the view.

"I think her parents gifted it to her. Maybe seven years ago? I can't quite remember, but I do know that she totally immersed herself in redesigning the acreage so she had a riding stable, bunkhouses and a modernized house. Her intensions were to work with underprivileged children. However, since Boris is now a part of her life, her focus has changed to breeding quarter horses and training them for barrel racing."

Waving her arms, Kim, wearing a mask, was at the top end of the lane and indicating where to park. She strode over, opened the passenger door and wrapped Ann in her arms as soon as she stood up.

"We are going to have a blast today. Boris has arranged for a small barrel-racing event. Are you familiar with this sport?"

"Not really. I simply know it has something to do with riding around barrels."

"This is a rodeo event in which a horse and rider attempt to run a cloverleaf pattern around pre-set barrels in the fastest time. It's usually an event for women. Boris is an exceptional trainer so our horses are highly sought after. Our two other trainers are top notch, too, and this afternoon, we're showcasing ten horses that are ready for competition. This is actually a sales event as well. Most of the horses are trained and ready to go to other horse farms. Potential buyers will be here with well-heeled wallets, I hope."

"I'm sorry, I didn't know you were working. I hope we're not in the way. Also, due to my condition, I can't be near other people."

"I'm a spectator as well. This is Boris's gig. The upside is, because it is a buyer's event, there's lots of food and booze. Also, I can't think of a better time to let you see how I spend my days. It's a big change from what I originally intended to do with the ranch, but I love it."

"Aren't you riding in the event?"

"Sweetheart, I'm too big and too heavy. Poor horse would buckle under me." Kim broke out in a loud guffaw and slapped Ann on the back. "Before we settle in to watch the event, I want to shown you our newest addition." Kim led them to a field that was some distance away from the paddock.

"Oh, Kim. It's so sweet. When was it born?"

"A week ago. Come. We have to get to the competition. I wanted to show you this wee foal but now, let's go." She led her guests across a grassy area to a pop-up canopy.

Boris rushed over to greet them but was diligent to stay a

proper social distance away.

"My dear friends, I'm delighted you found the time to join us. Kim will have to take care of you as I'm off to convince a few gentlemen and their ladies that they should spend their hard-earned dollars on my over-priced horses." Boris blew Ann an air kiss and waved his hand toward Ray then turned and strode off across to another tented area. Ray was thankful to see that Boris, too, was masked.

Directly in front of the canopy, a fence cordoned off the paddock where the competition was going to take place. Ann and Ray watched a group of people in jeans and leather jackets move from the other tent to lean against the fence. They were all holding what looked like champagne flutes.

"The fun is about to start. Grab a glass of bubbly and I'll explain what the riders are doing." Ann picked up a water bottle and Ray took a glass of beer and followed Kim to the fence. As they approached, they saw a rider move into a cordoned-off lane that led to the competition area where three barrels were positioned in a set pattern, known as a cloverleaf pattern.

"As you can see, the barrels are strategically placed. The rider must follow a specific course. The barrels are measured to be a set distance apart to force quick, difficult turns. The tighter the rider can round the barrel, the better their time. They are not to topple the barrel or they lose five seconds off their time. And five seconds in this game is a disaster. To get their mount around the course, the horse has to be very agile and sure-footed. The rider needs to give it the right amount of turning space. It's all about timing. The fastest time without a penalty is the winner."

Ann watched as the rider set off at an extremely fast pace and rode the course in what Ann thought was an extremely fast time.

"She's lagging. That horse can do a whole lot better." Kim was shaking her head, obviously disappointed in the resulting time, "Each buyer has an information sheet with the horse's stats so they know its history. They will note that this horse can do better."

As soon as the rider completed the course and exited the arena, another horse was at the starting point at the entrance to the corral.

"Oh my, what a beauty!" Ann was pointing at the new competitor. Its glossy chestnut coat gleamed, and a white blaze shot along its nose.

"Yes, Rankler is a beauty but between you and me, he's a wee bit temperamental. But he loves to compete. Hates having his hooves cleaned, though. Apt to bite your ass if you are not watching him. He's a great competitor. Just watch how he leans in to get around each barrel. He's not on the list to sell yet. He needs a few more months of training."

The trio watched the chestnut charge out of the starting gate heading for one of the three barrels. "They have to complete the pattern and the fastest time is the winner. If they knock over a barrel there is a five second deduction but if the barrel is touched but does not fall over there's no penalty. Oh, I think I already told you that."

"Wow. Look at him go! Go Rankler" Ann was shouting as she leaned over the fence. Rankler leaned almost sideways to round a barrel, straightened up and tore toward the next one. All of a sudden Ann grabbed Ray's sleeve and leaned into him.

"You okay, babe?" He eased Ann back to the tent and sat her in one of the chairs. He wrapped her in a blanket as he knew she would be chilled.

Ann gave Kim a weak smile.

"What can I do?" Kim was obviously concerned.

"Nothing. She'll be okay in a few minutes."

Ann nodded.

As soon as Ann felt better, she headed back to the fence to watch more racing. "Kim, I am so hooked on this sport. I hope I can come again. Are the horses expensive?"

"Depends. Ours are hefty prices because they outperform nearly all other breeders' horses. I think Rankler will likely go around a half a million."

"What?"

"Sweety, they can earn that much in a season. The stakes are high."

Ray watched Ann's colour fade and insisted they leave so she could get some rest.

"Listen, my friend. You let me know whatever you want. I need you as a friend and you have to get better. That fighting spirit of yours is your best asset right now." Kim spoke with assurance and walked along beside Ann and Ray as they went to their car.

"Thanks, Kim. I'll beat this rotten thing. I *will* beat this horrible disease."

Kim gave her another hug as Ann eased into the passenger seat.

"God, Ray. I could get hooked on that sport. Did you see Rankler lean almost sideways to round each barrel. It looked like he was going to fall over, yet he didn't. I swear he was smiling. I want to go to the next competition."

***

The next day was chemo day. The doctor had prescribed meds to prevent Ann from throwing up and to make the treatment easier. She was no sooner home with Snuggles cuddled into her lap rug, when Ann threw rug, cat and all and raced for the bathroom. The next few days were spent resting. The drugs had helped, but she still had some nausea and was very tired. The bloodwork came back with little improvement showing. Tired as she was, Ann researched everything she could find on barrel racing. She learned that an international competition was to be held in Ottawa in September. She intended to be well enough to attend.

The blood tests continued to show high levels of white count and Dr. Helms sat with Ann and Ray to explain. "Leukemia is a formidable and very aggressive disease. At this point, I am contemplating a bone marrow transplant. Unfortunately, none of your family and friends that were tested is a match. Because of your B-negative blood type, sometimes it's difficult to find the right donor. But we will. Right now, the donor bank does not have anyone. Do you by any chance have other relatives that might help?"

Ann looked at him with a blank expression as she shook her head. Hers was a small family. "I can put out an appeal on social media. That's all I can think off." Tears were streaming down her face.

Dr. Helms handed her a tissue. "There's another route we can go but a transplant is by far the best option."

Ray led a shaken Ann out of the office. He, too, was trembling. His whole life centred around his wife. The thought of losing her was devastating.

Weak and feeling defeated, Ann headed directly to bed when

they got home. She had almost dropped off when she sat up and called Ray. He came running, his eyebrows furrowed into a frown of concern.

Ann reached for him and looked directly into his eyes. "I didn't tell you this, but I received a strange note several weeks ago."

Ray was puzzled and began to think Ann was suffering delusions from the chemotherapy. He stroked her back and tried to ease her down onto the pillow.

"No! You must listen to me. I got a note in the mail from some man named Bert who claimed he might be my biological father."

"Honey. You're having some difficulty accepting the truth. I know the mind can play cruel tricks but trust me, you *are* hallucinating."

"No! Honestly! I'm not! At the time, I thought it was a prank and didn't pay a lot of attention, but I did try the phone number. Listen to me, Ray. If this is true, there might be another person to consider as a donor."

"I can't imagine your mother having an affair and that's the only way it could happen. She and Stan …"

"Listen to me, Ray. I asked Elsie if the name Bert — that's how he signed the note — meant anything to her. She denied it but her answer was hesitant. I think she was lying."

"I'm shocked. When did this happen and where's the letter?"

"Oh, God. I can't think."

Ray slipped into the bed beside Ann and held her close. Snuggles thought this the perfect time to pounce on Ann's legs and knead the covers. His purr was loud, cutting though the silence between his people. Ray's hand went automatically to stroke his back.

"It was the morning of the accident!" Ann was pushing to get up. I think I left it on my desk. I went to check where the phone number was located."

"Did you try the number?"

"Yes. And there was no answer. And the voicemail had not been activated. That's why I checked where the number was located."

"And where was it?"

"California, Sacramento area."

Ann was now easing into her slippers and attempting to stand. Ray had moved aside and Snuggles lay on his back waiting for tummy rubs, but none came. Realizing that his people were leaving, Snuggles scampered off the covers and jumped to the floor to follow.

Ann shuffled papers on her desk, checked to see if Google had saved her query, then sat down in disappointment. "I didn't use Google. I used the phone directory. I'm sure I didn't throw it out. But for the life of me, I can't find it."

"Okay. What did you do after you checked the phone number?"

"I went for my run. Then, of course, the whole world went crazy when that truck slammed into the car. I was so distracted, I must have thrown it out. I'm tired."

Ann returned to bed with Snuggles close behind. She ruffled his head as she closed her eyes.

Ray sat at Ann's desk, trying to absorb the information Ann had revealed. If this were true, there was another donor potential. This meant confronting Elsie. He knew that if this were a fact, it would deeply hurt Stan. Stan was the ultimate father, he adored Ann. She was his pride and joy. At first, he had not believed Ann, but now he did.

Ann slept for three hours and wakened feeling refreshed and hungry. She shuffled off to the kitchen with Snuggles following close behind. He sat beneath the cupboard where his treats were stored and looked pleadingly at Ann.

"Oh you little mooch. It sure didn't take you long to figure that one out." Ann reached for the bag of treats and set two on the floor for Snuggles. He downed them before she had the bag back in the cupboard and was looking at her, begging with imploring eyes.

"No. No more." Ann made herself a peanut butter sandwich, poured a glass of milk, and went in search of Ray. She found him on the patio, soaking up some of the early spring sunshine. She noted the forsythia was budding. Everything was coming to life. She set her snack on the picnic table, bent to give Ray a kiss on the cheek then sat in the chair beside him.

Snuggles ventured to the lawn. This was new territory and he investigated it with caution, taking short steps and sniffing as he went. A robin lifted from the grass and flew away. Snuggles froze in his tracks then charged after the bird that was now in full flight.

"Ah, the mighty hunter! He will get lots of exercise this summer. I sure hope he doesn't catch any of our beloved feathered friends. We must make sure he's never outside without us. Perhaps we should get a bell for his collar."

"That walk with Jason sure was rewarding."

Ann ate her sandwich and drank her milk. "I'm going to do the laundry then go for a run."

"Honey, you can't go for a run. How about we go for a walk around the block?"

"Damn this condition. I miss my run. Okay, a walk then." Ann went to put on her sweatshirt and a vest because it was cool out. The walk was interrupted several times with neighbours stopping to chat. A soft breeze drifted through the late afternoon, and Ann inhaled the sweet smells of earth and freshly mown grass.

"Ray, I have to ask Elsie again, but not having the letter, I have no idea how to reach this man. I don't know what else to do. It may be the only chance I have."

"You know this will devastate Stan."

Chapter 18

They walked on, the silence between them heavy with unspoken thoughts. When they got back to the house, Ann went to put the laundry in the dryer, pulled off her sweatshirt to throw in the next load. She stopped with her shirt midair, turned and ran back to the bedroom. Ray was coming out of the bathroom, nearly colliding with her. She hurried past him and began rummaging through her drawers.

"Ann. What are you doing?"

"I remember putting the letter in the back pocket of my jeans. Where the devil are they? I always hang them on the back of the closet door. But they're not there."

"Okay. Calm down. Did you wash them and put them somewhere else?"

Ann lashed out at Ray. "Why the hell would I do that? I always put them on the same hook. You didn't throw them out because they were old and you thought I might not be running again. Did you?"

"Ann, of course I wouldn't throw them out. To begin with, I avoid house chores whenever possible. Besides, I know they're your favourite running jeans. They've got to be here someplace. Try and think what you did when you changed after the accident."

Ann stared at him as her memory raced over her movements that morning. "I remember. I ripped them on a jagged piece of metal before I got out. The paramedic was able to push the pant leg up far enough to attend to my wound so she didn't have to cut the jeans."

Ann stood staring into the dresser mirror, scratching her head. "They're in the mending pile." She yelled and turned quickly and passed Ray as she went to a corner of the closet where she kept a basket with articles of clothing and other things that needed mending. This was a chore she disliked intensely so mending accumulated in a basket that she shoved to the back of the closet and often forgot about. She rummaged through the pile and pulled out her jeans. She swung them high in the air with a gleeful cheer.

"Yahoo! Success!"

She pulled the envelope from the back pocket and handed it to Ray.

He took Ann by the elbow and directed her to the bed and sat beside her. "I can't understand why you didn't tell me about this."

"Things got a little crazy that morning. I simply forgot." Ann's tone was smug.

Ray looked at the letter, picked up his cell and dialed the number. Again, it went unanswered and there was no voicemail. "We need to talk to Elsie."

Knowing Stan would be out the following morning at the curling club, Ann and Ray went over to see Elsie.

She denied knowing a Bert but her eyes were seeking a place to land and she started to rub the tips of her fingers. Ann explained about having received the letter and the importance of contacting him. Elsie listened in silence then broke down in tears before whispering. "Please don't tell Stan. It'll break his heart."

"What happened, Mom? I need to know."

Ann had spoken in anger, but seeing how distraught Elsie was, reached for her hand. The gesture was calming to both of them. One of understanding, not anger.

"It's not something I'm proud of. I love your father and always have. Please believe me. Nobody knows." Elsie was pleading through tear-streaked eyes. Both Ray and Ann nodded.

"If nobody knew then how did this Bert person know to contact me?"

Elsie leaned back then moved forward placing her arms along the table in a defeated motion. "I went to a convention. I went alone, the only person from our office. I was sitting in a session beside a man about my age. We started talking and found both of us were there alone. After the session, we decided to go for a drink. We were enjoying our conversation. We laughed and were totally connected. That drink turned into several. As you know, I do not handle alcohol well at all. One thing led to another and the next thing I remember was waking up in his hotel room. The obvious had happened. We were both embarrassed, me more than him, I think. We were apologetic and parted, intending to never to see each other again. We did exchange contact information though. Four weeks later, I realized I was pregnant. I wasn't concerned as Stan and I had had relations when I returned so I knew he could assume it was his. Years later, when we had not conceived again, Stan was tested and we learned that his sperm count was far too low to impregnate me. He expected this condition had occurred after I had conceived you. I knew different, but also felt it was prudent to never tell him. I still do not want to tell him."

"Okay, Elsie. Understood and I agree. But how did 'Bert' learn you were pregnant?"

"He found me a few years later when he was on a trip to Ottawa. He gave me a call, but I cut him short and in my haste to get rid of him, I blurted out that our encounter might have caused me to be pregnant. I yelled at him to stay away from me. I was so worried that he might tell Stan. I made him promise to never contact me again. He didn't."

"But why now and why through me?"

"I have no idea, but whatever happens, Stan must never know. Promise me you'll never tell him."

"Elsie, you know we have to find this Bert. Whoever he is and wherever he is. Ann's life depends on it. Once we do, and if he's a match, we'll convince him that Stan has to believe that he was found through the bone marrow donor registry. We had to talk to you to confirm that he was real."

Elsie reached for Ann. Her hands were trembling. "Please forgive me. A foolish night brought your father and me the best gift we could possibly have."

Ann's brows were furrowed and she spoke softly and sincerely. "I will not judge you. You have lived with this all my life, and it was and is your burden. Stan will always be my only father. Rest assured. This knowledge does not make me love you less. It does introduce a side of you that I never even guessed was there, but it doesn't change anything. I do love you." Ann lifted her mother's fingers that still rested on the table, and squeezed them. They talked for another hour before Ray saw Ann fading and knew she needed her afternoon rest.

***

In the car, they went over and over what had transpired that afternoon.

"This is weird! I can't imagine how you feel" Ray put on the left turn-signal and eased onto the 417 West.

"There's no way to describe how I feel. I'm shocked to learn that my suspicions were true. I'm also a little scared not knowing who this man is. I know we have no choice but to find him, but what if he's insane? Ray, I have no idea what genetics I might have inherited. What if we bring this man into our lives and regret it? Maybe we should try another way."

"Listen to me, Ann. Think about who your mother is. She is one steadfast woman. Even drunk as a skunk, I can't see her hooking up with a maniac. Besides, she was dead sober when they met. So forget all your drama and let's hope we can find this guy."

"But, love. I can't help but think there's likely something unpleasant that I'd inherit."

"You know your dad always wondered where your creative side comes from. He claims that neither he nor your mother had a smidgeon of creativity in their genes. Come on. Let's get you to bed. You're fading fast." Ray was pulling into the driveway. He pushed the garage door opener and drove inside and closed the door.

Ann stepped out of the car and had to grab the fender to steady herself.

"Dizzy?"

"Yep. Need my beddy."

When Ann was resting, Ray intended to try to locate this Bert individual. Once again, there was no answer when he dialed the number on the note. Thinking about what they knew, Ray had a light-bulb moment and called a friend of his, Reeve, who worked at Intel.

"Sorry, Ray, but I cannot use the system for personal reasons."

Once Ray explained the importance of finding this man,

Reeve agreed to see what he could find out. "Likely take a day or two but I'll get back to you, my friend."

Ann wakened screaming.

Ray rushed to the bedroom and quickly wrapped her in his arms. She was shaking and crying so hard she was choking.

"I was falling down a crevasse."

"Sweetheart, you had a nightmare. Take a deep breath and slowly release it. That's good. Now do that a couple of times again. Your heart is racing. You need to calm down."

"It was so real!"

"Trust me. You are in your own bed and you sure as heck are not falling anywhere."

Once Ann was breathing normally, she felt better and started to laugh. "Whew. That was frightening. Do you think it might be caused by the drugs?"

"Likely. Or it could simply be because you are experiencing trauma and concern about what is happening. Crap, I just might start having nightmares, too."

"That's all we need. Both of us to wake up screaming. Actually, now that I have settled down, I feel quite refreshed. Why don't we invite Brenda and Dan over for supper?"

"Do you think that's a good idea?

"I want to bring Brenda up to date on what's happening."

"Are you going to tell her about Bert?"

"Why not? She's my best friend. We don't keep secrets from each other."

"Yes, but it's not about you. It's about Elsie. We should respect her privacy. She has kept this secret for over forty years. I'm sure she would not want anyone else to know."

"I understand that, but I need to confide in Brenda and I know she will not tell a soul. Anyway, since I want to talk to her, I'm going to ask her over for dinner."

Ray agreed on the condition that he order in the meal from the local deli so Ann did not tire herself out cooking.

"Great idea!" Ann picked up her cell and called Brenda.

"Love to, but Dan won't join us as he has plans to horse around with some friends in the park. They're promising to wear masks and practise social distancing. This virus thing is changing the way we mingle. I'm glad we're in a chosen bubble and I don't have to wear a mask and can still give you a hug."

Brenda picked up the dinner Ray had ordered on her way over to Ann and Ray's. Ann had suggested a help-yourself type meal with chicken wings, onion rings, a huge Caesar salad and crusty garlic bread. Brenda stopped at the grocery store and added ice cream. She also brought a bottle of pinot noir.

All three were dressed in sweat suits so they could lounge in front of the TV as they ate. Ray had to pause the movie several times as there were lively exchanges of opinion regarding the acting, the timing, and many other elements they criticized about the production. Laughter was often interrupted with shouts of opposition to a point. This open and rowdy exchange was typical of their evenings together. What was not typical was that Ann seemed distracted.

"Ray, I am sick to death to see her like this. Have the doctors decided what to do next?"

"The chemo is not as successful as we expected so that's why we hoped one of the family or her friends would test positive as a donor. At this point there *are* no matches. Apparently, her genetics do not fall into the usual categories. Even her blood type is rare. We are pursuing another avenue though. It might be our last hope. The doctor indicated if we could not find a match, there was one other option, but the success rate is not as high as a matched donor. In the meantime, the doctor has decided to add another chemo treatment. Thank goodness she's taking a drug to counter the nausea. Brenda, I am trying to be brave but it's not easy."

"We may have found a relative in Sacramento."

Brenda nodded. "Seriously? So who is this mystery donor?"

"Are you ready for this? He's likely my biological father."

"What?"

"Long story, but Stan was never able to impregnate Elsie."

"So they found a sperm donor?"

"Sort of, but not quite. Elsie found one on her own. Stan doesn't know. He's sure I'm due to his own performance." Ray stared at Ann and nodded in agreement at her explanation. Ann continued to fill Brenda in on all the details.

"Well I can't get over the likelihood of such a thing. I'm shocked. Let's hope you find this person is he is not only compatible, but agrees to be a donor."

"As I mentioned, he lives in California and we have not been able to contact him as yet. We will keep trying until we do. Can you believe it, Brenda? Never in my life would I have thought such a thing was possible. I am nervous as can be about meeting this person."

"We will deal with that when the time comes. There are so many things to consider. Once we find him, and if he does agree to be a donor, the logistics of getting him here are mind boggling. We will have to arrange his airfare and accommodation. I'm sure I have enough credits that I can swing a free trip."

"Hey, I could do with a free trip!" Brenda offered her

apologies and said she had to leave as she had another busy day ahead. "Keep me in the loop. I hope you find this Bert, whoever he is, soon."

Ann was exhausted and opted to stay on the sofa rather than see Brenda out. Ann promised her that she would be kept up to date on all new information. Brenda turned and gave both Ann and Ray a big hug before leaving.

As soon as Brenda left, Ann went to bed and Ray settled into the recliner. Snuggles jumped up on Ray's lap, rubbing his head against Ray's chin demanding to be noticed. He had stayed under the bed while Brenda was there. He was shy around strangers. Now he wanted Ray's full attention. Ray smiled as he heard the loud purrs of satisfaction.

His phone buzzed.

"Hello."

"Hope it's not too late to call." Ray recognized Reeve's raspy smoker's voice. "I think I found your guy."

"Seriously! So fast?"

"It wasn't hard. He's still in California. I don't know why he doesn't answer his phone because it's still active. You're right, however, he hasn't activated the voicemail. His name is Bert Hansen and he works at a film studio. Amazing Video. He's a production manager. You can likely call him there."

"Reeve, you are one hell of a guy. I can't thank you enough. Do you have the number?"

"I'll text it over to you. Please let me know how this goes and keep me abreast of Ann's progress."

"This information might be exactly what she needs. Again, many thanks."

Knowing that California was a three-hour time difference,

Ray took the chance that a filming studio might still be open at 5:00 Pacific Time so dialed the number Reeve had sent over.

"Amazing Video, Angela speaking."

"Angela, I am trying to reach Bert Hansen. Would he be available?"

"Please hold. I will transfer you."

Ray took a deep breath and sent up a prayer as he waited for the call to be answered.

"Hey, Bert Hansen here. How can I help?"

Very carefully, Ray explained who he was. He got a hesitant "uh" from the other end. "Please don't hang up. This call is very important."

"I had no intention of hanging up." Bert's west-coast accent was pronounced yet soothing as Ray started to tell him why he had phoned.

"You listen here, my friend. I have no other children so we have to do whatever is necessary to make Ann well. Just tell me where to go. I'll go to Ottawa tomorrow. If I might be a match for this little lady, I will do anything needed to help. I will make the travel arrangements as soon as we disconnect." Bert was talking in rapid sharp sentences.

"You don't have to come here to be tested. That can be done right there."

"Nope. I'm going to Ottawa, I want to meet Ann, regardless. I need to know if she's my biological daughter. Although I'm pretty sure she is."

"Bert, that information must stay confidential. Elsie doesn't want Stan to have any inkling that he's not her father."

"Got that. I won't breathe a whisper about it. Like you said, I'll readily confirm that you found me on the donor list. But there's also another reason I need to talk to Ann."

Ray gave Bert his phone number and promised to answer when called. He indicated that texting was the best option to connect with him. Bert did not want Ray to book a flight and did not want to be picked up at the airport. He assured Ray that he would make his own flight and hotel arrangements. Bert promised to call once he was settled. Ray felt that Bert had reacted too quickly and the call had been strange. He couldn't imagine how Bert would be able to catch a flight that quickly. In spite of his doubts, he hoped that Bert meant what he said.

Chapter 19

When Ray set his phone down, he thought about how to tell Ann. It was with caution that Ray recounted his conversation with Bert, trying not to get her set up for a big letdown.

When he peeked into the bedroom, Ann was fast asleep. He decided to wait until morning to share the news.

Around five o'clock, Ann wakened screaming again. Ray reached over and cuddled her. Once again, she was shaking but not crying.

"Okay, my love. You were dreaming again. Want to tell me what it was about?"

"I don't remember except that I was trapped in a cement cubicle. It wasn't as frightening as falling, but I was starting to panic when you wakened me."

"If you are completely awake, I have some exciting news." Ray filled Ann in on his conversation with Bert.

"But why is he coming all the way here? That doesn't make sense. Do you think he's all right? Or do you think he might be a weirdo?"

"He sounded okay but it's strange that he decided to book a flight and come right away. He said something about needing to meet you and tell you something."

"I guess we'd better alert Elsie that he's coming."

"Let's not. Let's wait to see what he's like and what he really wants. I'm skeptical about what we might encounter. He might be a complete nut-case. Anyway, it's only another day then we'll have a better idea what to expect."

Keeping Bert's pending arrival secret was gnawing at Ann. There were so many unanswered questions. Her mind was in overdrive. In the event that he did arrive and meant what he said about being a donor, Ann knew she had to arrange the bone marrow test. Once the clinic was open, she arranged an appointment for Bert to be tested for compatibility the day following his arrival. She booked two times, one early in the morning and the other early afternoon. She had no idea what kind of schedule he would keep and there was the three-hour difference between California and Ottawa so he might sleep in late.

Ann was now very tired all the time. She had not been sleeping well and the nightmares were disconcerting. The very thought that she would be meeting her biological father — one she didn't even know she had until very recently — was filling her head with all kinds of notions. All day, she tried to envision how tall he was, did he have a beard, was his hair grey, and most of all, would she feel an emotional connection. She was terrified that the resemblance between them might be so evident that Stan would guess right away. Somehow, she managed to get through the day. Ray and Ann talked well into the night and tossed and turned the rest of it.

* * *

Ann rose early and once the coffee pot was on, decided to bake a coffee cake. By having to concentrate on the ingredients, she was able to pass the time until Ray wandered into the kitchen.

"Is that my favourite breakfast I smell?"

"Just about to come out of the oven. Coffee's ready. Want me to pour you a cup?"

"First, I want a big kiss from my best gal." Ray wrapped his arms around Ann and drew her to him. He held her cheeks and planted a noisy smacker on her lips.

Flushed and smiling, Ann reached for a mug and filled it with coffee. "Today is either going to be momentous or a bust. I do hope and pray Bert is for real. Somehow, I believe he is. I want to believe."

"Don't get your hopes up. Life has a way of coming crashing down when your hopes are too high. Did I tell you yet this morning that I love you?"

"No, do tell."

Ray kissed Ann's neck and whispered his love into her ear. Wriggling free, Ann opened the oven and took out a perfect coffee cake. The kitchen was filled with smells of cinnamon and freshly baked aromas. Ray quickly put plates, knives and butter on the table while Ann upended the cake onto a platter. They were so busy, the ringing of the phone made both of them jump and they bumped into each other scrambling for it.

"Rogers residence." Ray was withholding a giggle and Ann had her hand over her mouth so she wouldn't burst out laughing. "Hi, Elsie. What's up?"

"I thought I would go to the Byward Market and wondered if Ann was interested in joining me." Ray put the phone on speaker so Ann could hear Elsie, too.

"Not today, Elsie. Thanks for asking, but Ray and I have other plans."

"Oh, what are you two doing?"

"We may have to have a meeting with someone. We're waiting to hear when and where. I'll tell you all about it the next time I see you. Have fun at the market."

Ray disconnected the call and looked at Ann. "Nervous?"

"Very. When that call came, I was afraid it would be Bert. This is so nerve wracking."

"Put on the news, I want to hear if the rest of the world is still out there."

"You watch the news. I'm going to have a bath and wash my hair."

While Ann was in the tub, Bert called. Ray agreed to meet for lunch at the Chateau Laurier. Bert gave Ray his suite number. The restaurant was closed but room service still was offered.

Ann was soaking in the tub with her eyes closed when he went into the bathroom. Lazily she opened them but sat bolt upright when Ray told her about the call.

"He's for real." Ann's hushed whisper was full of awe.

"It appears so. Mmm. Don't you smell delicious?"

"Not now, Ray. I have to dry my hair and decide what to wear. What does one wear when one meets their biological father for the first time? Shit, I'm so nervous."

Snuggles was wrapping himself around Ray's ankles as Ray was helping Ann reach for a towel. He picked up Snuggles in one hand and handed Ann a towel with the other. "Perhaps you had better have a rest so you don't flake out at lunch."

"Good point. I'll dry my hair then lie down for an hour."

When Ann got up, she pulled one outfit after the other out of her closet. She finally settled on a simple dress of sage green. The flared skirt swayed as the fine woollen fabric moved to her rhythm. She applied makeup with care, settled on gold hoop earrings and picked out a soft, beige, cashmere car coat. Looking in the mirror, she saw an image of a figure that appeared calm and in control. She was anything but.

She picked up her purse and headed for the car. Ray had already taken it out of the garage and was waiting on the driveway. Traffic was light and they arrived at the Chateau before the time specified. The Chateau Laurier was in the city's downtown core, at the intersection of Rideau Street and Sussex Drive and had been designed in a French, gothic-revival, chateauesque style to complement the adjacent Parliament buildings. The hotel sat over the Colonel By valley, home of the Ottawa locks of the Rideau Canal and also overlooked the Ottawa River.

There was lots of parking available so Ann and Ray went in the back door, walked along the hallway and headed for an elevator. Ray smiled as he walked behind Ann who had bolted down the hallway. Ann's low-heeled pumps made walking easy, and Ray hustled to keep up with her. Even though she had lost a great deal of weight, to him she was still beautiful in every way and very sexy. He had chosen to wear his grey suit with a navy shirt and silver tie. They rounded the corner to a bank of elevators, and got into a waiting one and pushed the button for the top floor. When Ray knocked softly, a tall grey-haired man appeared.

"You must be Bert," Ray had his hand extended.

A captivating smile spread across the face of the man standing there. "Might be. Ray? And you must be Ann."

Ray overheard the rich Californian accent when he spoke.

Bert reached for Ann's hand and looked deep into her eyes then bent to kiss her hand. Then he raised his head and gazed intensely at her before he broke into a radiant smile. His easy manner and captivating grin made a moment that might have been awkward, a relaxed one. Bert indicated for them to follow him. "In a way I'm glad the dining room is closed. This way we can have privacy."

A table was set for three and Bert led them to it and held a chair out for Ann and slid it in as she sat. Ray eased into another chair across from the one Bert chose, never taking his eyes off Bert. Ann clenched her fists then loosened them, trying to appear calm when, in fact, she was as tense as could be. No one spoke for what seemed agonizing minutes then everyone started talking at once. This broke the tension and they all laughed. The unknown hung like heavy shrouds making the pressure of their silence fill with expectation.

Finally, Bert cleared his throat and leaned forward. "Ray, you asked me if I had other children who might be possible donors. My answer was 'no'. I can certainly explain the reason why. Shortly after I left the convention where I met Elsie, I met Patrick. The attraction between us was immediate and mutual. We have been a couple ever since. We are a gay couple, a gay married couple. Our devotion to each other makes each of us complete. I'm sure Elsie will be able to put our night of indiscretion behind her and Stan would never suspect foul play. It was an encounter, not a relationship."

"Wow! You're gay? I hadn't thought of that! I'm totally blindsided. That being the case, you're right. Dad will never suspect a gay man to be my biological father. Even though this seems complicated, the fact that you are gay does make matters easier. Bert, you have to understand how I appreciate your coming all this way. As Ray mentioned, it was not necessary, you could have been tested in California."

"I know. However, even though I hope and pray that my tests will qualify me as your donor, Ann, I would have come regardless. I wanted to meet you. Your illness gives me an opportunity, I hope, to bring you life for a second time."

"This is kind of weird sitting here talking to a stranger trying to find a connection, trying to see if I resemble you. We certainly don't share noticeable physical features. I tried all day yesterday to imagine what I might have inherited from you. Certainly not your beard! You know, this is very awkward and I'm extremely uncomfortable dealing with this new relationship."

"Oh, Ann. I'm glad you put it that way because I do hope we can develop a relationship. Due to my lifestyle, I have no other children. Patrick and I chose not to adopt because we were starting the company and we were working sixteen hours a day. In the long run, it paid off."

"You own a video company?"

"Corporate videos and advertising stuff."

"You're not just the production manager, are you?"

"Patrick and I are partners and own a rather lucrative business."

"Ah. So I now understand how you were able to book a last-minute flight. They are so expensive."

"Actually, I didn't. We have our own plane. Our business requires us to move around a lot. There's another reason I wanted to come, to meet you of course, and to fill you in on who I am. Amazing Video is a high-end filming company that does specifically designed videos for corporations and wealthy individuals. It's a highly successful company and Patrick and I are worth a potful of money."

Bert leaned back and let out a chuckle. "I wish I was recording the expressions on your faces right now. You are truly bug-eyed."

"Here's a thought." Ray coughed, put his arm around Ann

and squeezed her upper arm. "Since you are gay, Stan could meet you and never for one minute suspect that you were Ann's biological father. He would simply assume that we found you on the donor list. I don't know if you want to see Elsie, but if you do, this will make it easier."

"You can trust me to never whisper a word about how I came into your life. However, I would like to speak with Elsie. Patrick and I need to ask her something and clarify what we are contemplating."

"Can I ask what that is?"

"No. And in the meantime, how do I go about getting tested?"

"Oh. Yes. I forgot to tell you that I booked two times tomorrow. We weren't sure, with the time difference between here and California, what would work for you. I booked nine in the morning and one in the afternoon. Take your pick." Ann took out her phone to cancel the appointment that would not be used.

"Morning works for me. Where do I go?"

"We'll pick you up and drive you to the cancer clinic. That's likely the best option. The test is immediate so if you match, we'll arrange for the next step while we're there."

Lunch arrived minutes later. Bert had ordered a large platter of seafood, cooked meats, salad, and an array of crackers. A bottle of pinot noir was chilling in a bucket.

Chapter 20

Conversation turned from Ann's medical problems to getting to know each other. Bert had already read Ann's books and was complimentary. "Once you are over this scare and on the road to recovery, I might have some connections in California that can bump up your sales."

"My agent would handle that and be delighted to see increased sales. Hey, if you make me a best-selling author, I can buy Rankler." Ann laughed and rolled her eyes to the ceiling.

"What the heck is a rankler?"

"To make a long story short, Ann's friend, Kim, has a ranch that breeds quarter horses and trains them for barrel racing. Ann and I visited the ranch for the first time last Tuesday and she was smitten, not only with the sport, but took a liking for one particular horse. Rankler is still young and needs lots of training, but has the potential of being one of their best animals. Ann simply fell in love with him."

"However, right now, the physical effort to watch a competition is trying, as I tire so easily, but I can't wait to go back. Kim is such a dear and her fiancé, Boris, is so knowledgeable about horses."

"You won't believe this, and you'll get a kick out of it, but I'm an avid spectator of barrel racing. Over the last fifteen years, I've sponsored many a rider in the United States and across Europe. Maybe genetics do come into play here. Maybe this is an inherited gene. Once we know what the test results are, and what transpires next, you will have to take me to the ranch and introduce me to Kim and Boris. He's not Boris Rychek is he?"

"Yes! How do you know him?"

"He's highly regarded in Europe. I didn't realize he was here in Canada. He has been around the barrel racing circuit since forever. I met him a few times at social gatherings after competitions. Great guy!

"Now, tell me about your mother. We did touch base once after we met at the conference but then she asked me to never contact her again. I respected her wishes."

"We know. She told us. We haven't told her about you being here yet. One, it happened so quickly and two, we were not certain how to tell her. Or if we deemed you a problem."

"Oh. Is that what you think I am?"

Ray looked at Ann and without saying a word they both knew each other's thoughts. "I don't see a problem so we *will* tell Elsie. She and Stan are retired, live a comfortable, uncomplicated lifestyle, and enjoy being together. Both are in good health. They were devastated about my diagnosis and fuss over me constantly. I know Mom is a little overbearing because she loves me so feels she needs to, but it does get stifling on occasion. Mom is an avid cook, especially desserts and since I've been sick, she brings over delicacies several times a week. Our freezer is full, and Ray and I slip the extras to Brenda and Dan."

Bert had a puzzled expression on his face. "Brenda and Dan?"

"Brenda's my best friend in the world. She is a tiny powerhouse who owns and operates a concrete company. She's a single mother to a seventeen-year-old son, Dan. She opted to raise him alone, so Ray is like a surrogate father. They're our extended family. Stan and Elsie treat them like family, too."

"You asked me about Patrick. When I returned to work after the conference where I met your mother, a new employee had joined the staff in the communications department at Canada Post's Mississauga branch. There was an instant connection. Before Patrick, I had no idea why I did not feel any attraction for any of the women I met. Forgive me, but Elsie was again, another encounter that did not offer me any romantic desires. It was more because we were at the conference by ourselves that we connected. We ended up in bed because we liked each other's company and had had far too much to drink."

"I know. Elsie told me."

Ray looked at Ann and knew the signs. "Bert, I have to get this lady home. She's about to crash. We'll call you later."

"That's fine. I have some plans for this afternoon. Let's leave it for today and you can pick me up tomorrow morning as planned."

With that, everyone rose and bid their farewells.

***

When Ann wakened from her nap, she phoned Elsie. "Are you sitting down?"

"No, dear. I'm watering my plants. Why?"

"Um. I think you'd better sit down. We may have a donor for a bone marrow transplant."

"That's wonderful, dear. I'm nearly beside myself with worry as it is but this might be the solution to that terrible invasive cancer. I just can't get my head around how rapidly you are getting worse. You've always been so healthy and full of energy. Now you're always tired, almost frail. I simply don't know how to deal with it. Your dad's the same. We're so very worried. Okay. Now I'm sitting. Tell me what this is all about."

"The likely donor is Bert."

Dead air on the other end of the line led Ann to ask. "Mom? Are you still there?"

"Yes." Elsie's breathing was short and rapid. "I — How?"

"Do you remember me telling you about the letter I received? And confronting you with needing to know if he *was* my biological father? Well. We tracked him down. There's so much to tell you. He flew into Ottawa yesterday. We had lunch together today. He wants to see you."

"That's impossible. Your dad can't know. Ann. You promised that your dad would never know." Elsie was frantic.

"Actually, Mom. Should dad meet him, he would never guess in a million years."

"How can you say that? There might be some resemblance between you and him?"

"You know something? There's not a bit. Nada. But here's why you needn't worry. Right after you and he met, Bert met a man by the name of Patrick and fell deeply in love."

"He's gay?"

"Yes. He and Patrick have been a couple since then, for over forty years."

"But how can that be? What he and I did wasn't something a gay man would do."

"According to Bert, he kept trying to find love and was always disappointed in his reaction to feeling a romantic relationship. With you, or any of the other women he met. When Patrick came into the picture and became a part of his life, he found his true love. They moved to California where they would be readily accepted, and got married. Not only are they married, but they're business partners, too. They started a small video company that specializes in specific clients. They have done very well for themselves and have a successful business."

"I'm still confused. How did you convince him to come?"

"There was no need. He insisted and arrived the night before last."

"And when you met him, what did you think?"

"He's a charming man but I've made it very clear that being my biological father does not give him any entitlement."

"I'm flabbergasted!"

"He would like to see you. I know this could be awkward but … Hold on. I have another call from the doctor. I'll call you back."

Elsie sat holding the watering can and staring out the window. Her phone beeped twice.

"I'm back. He was simply confirming our appointment for tomorrow morning. If Bert is a match, he'll undergo further blood tests and a physical exam in order to ensure that the donation is safe for both him and me. Once confirmed as medically eligible, we will start pre-transplant treatments to prepare us for the transplant."

"What does that mean, dear?"

"Apparently, to prepare for a stem cell transplant, the chemotherapy to kill the diseased cells and malfunctioning bone marrow I have been receiving will prepare *me* for the donation. If Bert is a march, he will undergo some additional tests to ensure *he* is healthy and not carrying any likely disease. Then a short surgical procedure is performed under anesthesia in which hollow needles withdraw stem cells from the bone marrow at the back of his pelvic bones. Then these stem cells are put into my bloodstream. The transplanted stem cells find their way to my marrow where they begin producing new, healthy blood cells."

"Let's hope and pray he's a match. I am completely thrown

by all this, but will be ready for whatever it takes to get you better. You know, we love you so much. When will you know if he's a match?"

"We have an appointment tomorrow morning. I think the results are almost immediate. I will learn more then. I know all this is upsetting for you, but trust me, your indiscretion will never be revealed to Dad and please think about meeting Bert. You will not regret it. Even if he's not a match, please consider at least meeting for coffee. I love you, Mom. Bye."

Chapter 21

When Ann got off the phone with Elsie, she called Brenda and filled her in on what was happening.

"My dear girl, I have to have all the details."

"Long story. Come over for dinner and I'll tell you all about him."

"Only if I can bring the food. There's no way you're cooking. You need to conserve all your energy for getting better. Of course, I'm coming. Wild horses couldn't keep me away from hearing all about all this."

"Wrong. Don't bring food. I need to keep busy so I don't fret and cooking is one thing I can do that doesn't tire me out. Ray can do the shopping and house cleaning but I love to claim the kitchen as my own. Must be my mother's genes. Is meatloaf okay?"

"You know it's one of my favourites. I'll leave Dan with pizza, his fav. Crap, Ann. Now I will be distracted for the rest of the day. I can't wait to hear all about your new father and how you reacted when you met him."

Brenda closed her phone and stared at it. Her own circumstances and how she had concealed who Dan's father was, dominated her thoughts. "So Elsie hid a secret, too." The words spilled out.

"Pardon ma'am? Were you talking to me?" Randy was returning from the yard with a request form for concrete.

He handed it to Brenda as she was shaking her head to his question.

The rest of the day seemed to pass in slow motion but when she locked up, she was glad it had been another busy day.

Finally, when she left, she headed for Stittsville. The traffic was stop and go, typical for that time of the day. Sirius was playing country and western. Brenda sang along with gusto. She knew most of the songs and this helped distract her from both the traffic and what Ann might tell her. She pulled off at Fernbank Plaza intending to get some flowers.

***

Brenda arrived with a bouquet of tulips and gave Ann a big hug when she found her busy in the kitchen.

"God, Ann. This is so unbelievable. Do tell all. I can't wait a minute longer."

Ann stepped away from the stove, put her hands on Brenda's shoulders, stared her in the eyes and laughed. "My dearest friend, you are not going to believe what I am about to tell you."

She quickly filled Brenda in on all the details, including what would happen the next morning.

"I'm thrilled that you may have a donor but so shocked at who he is. This is like something out of one of your novels. I can't imagine how Elsie feels right now. When can I meet him? Do you look like him? When will you know if he's a match?"

"Stop jabbering! You have far too many questions. The results are almost immediate. Stop with the questions. You know, Brenda, I'm still in a daze. This whole thing is mind blowing. I simply can't think of him as a father, but he is definitely a very nice man. Even if he's not a match, I have a feeling he'll hang around for a bit. So yes, I think you should meet him. He wants to be a part of my life and that being the case, you are an important part. I'm not sure I'm comfortable with being closely aligned. On the other hand, I'm not too unhappy about it."

The evening was short as Ann tired easily and had to be at her best the next morning. Brenda left shortly after supper and Ray and Ann watched the early news before Ann left Ray to his devices and she headed off to bed.

***

Ann got up early and wandered into the kitchen to have breakfast. Snuggles hung around her feet as if he knew that Ann was dealing with jangled nerves. Ann managed to eat a little but was not able to finish her cereal. She poured out her half-empty coffee cup and went to get dressed. She decided to be comfortable and grabbed a pair of designer jeans and a dust-of-roses cashmere sweater. She only applied the lightest of makeup, fearing she might be driven to tears again. Ray was having a shower as she sat at her dresser, filled with hope and dread at the same time. When Ray was dressed and had breakfast, they were ready to head for the hotel.

When Ann and Ray arrived at the hotel, Bert was already waiting at the front. "Morning, folks. This is the big tell this morning. I can't say how many messages I sent to the gods to make me a match." He gave Ann a peck on the cheek. "I feel very positive about this. Patrick is sending up all sorts of prayers to his gods, too."

"Don't for one minute think my gods haven't been bombarded with requests, too!"

Once at the hospital, Bert was ushered in right away and Ann and Ray waited in the hall. There were chairs, but Ray paced in one direction, Ann in the other.

Two hours later, Dr. Helms came in with a big smile on his face. "We are good to go!"

Ray jumped up and threw his arms around the doctor.

"We will keep Bert in overnight to run a few more tests and if all goes well, we'll do the transplant tomorrow afternoon. I know it's quick, but I don't want to postpone it. Your condition is rapidly deteriorating and you have had all the chemo that you need to be prepared. My team is here and can be ready."

"Can I ask what the success rate is, Doc?"

"Of course, Ray. I'm surprised we didn't discuss this earlier. Transplants have a much higher success rate with a seventy- to ninety-percent survival rate with a matched donor. In Ann's case, a bone marrow transplant is by far the best bet for a potential cure. During the procedure, Bert's healthy blood-forming cells will be transfused into Ann's bone marrow where they can begin to manufacture healthy cells into her bloodstream. Bert might experience some lower back discomfort, fatigue, throat pain, muscle pain — even insomnia — but he is more than aware of the risks. However, most donors recover well and are back to their normal routine within several days. Ann should start seeing a steady return to normal blood counts, depending on the possible variants, in about two to six days, then over the next two months, a steady improvement. Ann, in most cases you would be hospitalized so we can keep track of your progress, but since you live so close, I think you can be at home and that will be better for you. You'll need to visit the transplant centre daily for a number of days, and Ray. If you see anything that you deem negative, you need to rush Ann over here right away."

"Thank goodness we found Bert."

"We are fortunate that he is such a good match and that he practises a healthy lifestyle. I know that the story about finding him is worrisome to your mother, but I assure you, I'll never breathe a word to your father."

"Thanks, Doctor. I expect you are confirming then that he is my biological father."

"There can be no doubt."

"Okay." Ann wrapped her arms around her chest clutching at her shoulders. She started to shake. Learning that Bert was her biological father was hard to absorb, yet she was delighted that the bloodwork revealed that he was a good match for a bone marrow transplant. "Thanks, Doctor Helms. I guess we leave Bert with you, then. What time should we be here tomorrow?" Ann's voice was quivering.

"First thing in the morning. There's some necessary prep work before the procedure. I'll see you then."

Ann and Ray walked out into a downpour. They made a dash for the car and fell into their seats.

"Ann. You have no idea how relieved I am. I have lived in fear of losing you. Now life looks promising." He leaned over and held Ann's face in his hands, tears streaming down his face. "You are the love of my life."

"Let's go for a nice long drive."

"In the rain!"

"Okay then. Let's see if Mom baked today. I need to give her the news and a head's up about what to expect."

When they arrived at Elsie and Stan's, they found two very worried people. Once the news was shared, it was as if a dark phantom cloud had been sucked out of the room.

"Anything to eat, Mom? I'm starved."

"Lordy. I haven't given food a thought. Let's head over to Luigi's for spaghetti."

"Not possible. All the restaurants are closed. However, we

can order take-out."

Everyone was in accord and as soon as Stan returned with their order, they were digging into plates piled high with spaghetti and sipping wine, with the exception of Ann. With glasses raised high, they toasted to the success of the transplant.

"Where did you find this guy?" Stan asked between mouthfuls.

Ann hesitated then Ray gave her a nod.

"He showed up in California. It seems he's a video mogul and has mega bucks. He owns his own plane so was able to come on a day's notice. We're very fortunate to have found him."

"Well I want to meet this guy and shake his hand. Does he have any idea how important his involvement really is?"

"Stan? This guy is totally enamoured with Ann. I think he would adopt her if he could."

Elsie looked at Ray, her eyes as large as billiard balls. She threw her serviette on the table and burst out laughing. "Well with all that money, why not?"

After leaving Ann's parents' house, Ray and Ann did go for that long drive but simply to pass the hours. Each minute seemed to drag on and on.

"I do believe this is the longest day in my life." Ann wiped condensation off the side window. "Look Ray. Pull over. I want you to take my picture in front of that tree. It's a flowering crab in full bloom."

Indeed, the deep pink blossoms were alive with bees buzzing from branch to branch.

Ann laughed. "This is an expectation of warm weather and new life, Ray. I'm taking it as a promise of new cells blooming in my system."

Chapter 22

At sunup the next morning, Ray and Ann arrived at the hospital. Ann was whisked away and with a wave she disappeared down the hall.

"Excuse me. Are you Ray Rogers?"

Ray turned to see a tall slim man dressed in wrinkled cargo pants and a long-sleeved navy shirt open at the neck with a red silk scarf at his throat.

"I am." Ray waited for the man to identify himself.

"I'm Patrick. I flew in last night to be here with Bert. I'm pleased to meet you." With his tanned hand he reached toward Ray and smiled.

Ray automatically took the hand while taking in Patrick's tall frame and perfect posture. "Welcome to Canada."

"It's freezing out there! I'm used to Sacramento being on the cool side, but this is bone chilling. What I'm wearing is far too light. I'm going to have to buy some warm clothes. Any suggestions where I should go?"

"Listen. We could go right now because there's nothing we can do here for several hours. I can take you to one of our upscale stores, Holt and Renfrew. By the time we drive across town, they should be open. I'm sure they'll have something to your liking."

"As long as it's warm. Good. Let's go. I can leave my rental here, can't I?"

"Of course."

The two men set off while Ann and Bert underwent the bone marrow pre-transplant procedure. Traffic was a mess, so the stores were indeed open when they finally arrived downtown.

They parked underground and took the elevator to the first floor. Ray knew he had chosen well when he watched Patrick buy, not only a coat but he replaced his silk scarf with a cashmere one. He found several other items, too.

"Man! This is a fashion paradise! Won't I be the envy of all my friends in California."

"I never thought of Canada as a fashion setter, but I guess our styles are different from yours. Definitely warmer." Ray raised his eyebrows when the cash register showed the total amount of Patrick's purchases.

They opted to grab a lunch in the food court before returning to the hospital.

By the time Patrick and Ray pulled into the parking lot, they had become easy with each other. When they entered the waiting area, the receptionist signalled them and told them they could visit Ann and Bert. They followed her directions to where Ann and Bert were resting. The door to the room was open and they were sitting in reclining beds chatting away.

"You seem proud of yourselves." Ray walked quickly up to Ann and gave her a warm hug. Patrick did the same with Bert. "When can you get out of here?"

"Me? Probably within an hour or so if there's no sign of fever or extreme discomfort." Bert pointed to Patrick. "Been shopping have you? This man is clothes crazy."

"Well that explains his pleasure in finding several outfits. The credit card index rose a point or two when he cashed out."

Bert burst out laughing.

"Bert, I have to take you there. Wonderful choices. Ray certainly knows where to go."

"Holt and Renfrew's out of my league, but somehow I

thought Patrick might find what he liked there."

"You took him to Holts? My goodness, you'd better not have bought anything for yourself."

"No, but we had a good time."

Patrick and Ray laughed.

Ann explained that she would not be able to leave the hospital. Apparently, she would feel weak and might experience extreme nausea.

"Bert wants to see Mom. I'm not sure she feels the same, but she has agreed. I suggested we all meet in Bert and Patrick's suite for a late breakfast at the Chateau tomorrow morning, if all is okay, and I can get out of here."

Doctor Helms walked in at that time and overheard Ann. "Sorry Ann, but you have to stay in a germ-free environment for the first few weeks. I know you do not have children, so I am proposing that since you live so close to the hospital, you can go home. That being said, for the next two weeks you'll have to avoid visitors and the ones you do have will have to be masked. I'm suggesting that you allow Bert and your parents only. If no infections rear their ugly heads in the next few weeks, we will reassess what activities you can do. Frankly, your immune system will be fragile for about two years. Tomorrow, if you promise to be a good girl, Ray can take you home."

Ann slowly stood up and tried to walk a few steps. She realized immediately that she was way too wobbly so sat right back down.

The doctor checked the temperatures of both Ann and Bert. "You probably feel a bit woozy right now but that will likely disappear by this evening. I suggest you take it really slow even if you feel you want to fly. After this procedure, patients often feel so elated that they think they want to celebrate. Please be careful. Bert. You might want to take it easy, too, but you can go home."

"Home is a bit far, but I will hunker down at the hotel."

"Good. If you experience anything other than a bit of a sore back and stiff joints, call my office. We seldom see the donor experience any side effects, but I like to err on the side of caution."

Bert stood, being careful to ease to standing position, took one step then another. Patrick held Bert's arms to steady him and guided him out.

"Well it looks like breakfast at our house. Again, it will have to be a late breakfast as I understand that the lab will check my blood before I am released."

Ray stayed with Ann for the rest of the afternoon. He returned the following morning to take her home after she'd had a good night and the bloodwork was completed.

"I have to come here for seven o'clock in the morning every day for two weeks for a checkup. They should take about an hour. When everyone arrives for breakfast this morning, I'll venture into the kitchen for a few minutes, staying well away, then go back to my bed. This is awkward, but Bert is anxious to see Elsie, promising to be discrete. As a fair warning, she insists that Stan be there. This will be the first time Mom and Bert have seen each other in nearly forty years."

"Bert does not want to expose you to any danger, but wants Patrick to be there. I agreed as long as he keeps a fair distance away from you."

***

Elsie had been unusually quiet while she and Stan got ready to meet Bert. She took extra pains to look her best. The cream-coloured pantsuit set off her slim figure. She chose a simple, collarless, turquoise blouse and wore gold earrings and a chunky, gold, chain necklace. She smiled at the image in her mirror. Stan, his typical casual self, wore black slacks with a shirt slightly patterned with autumn leaves. He refused to wear a tie, but topped up his outfit with a tweed jacket.

"Well, my dear. We are ready." He held open the car door for Elsie, helped her carefully set the freshly baked muffins and bread on the back seat, then once she was settled, got in and drove off. Elsie didn't say a word all the way to Ann's. They drove along Heron Road, letting cars pass them, and making small talk and admiring the blossoms.

Stan and Elsie arrived first. As soon as Ray met them, he sniffed wonderful smells that came from the items Stan and Elsie cradled in their arms. Ray filled them in on Ann's checkup then Bert and Patrick arrived and walked in without knocking. Ray undertook introductions as if no one had met before. Elsie and Bert played their role to perfection shaking hands as they greeted each other. Ann met them in the dining room, with mimosas. Everyone reached for one except Bert who was on antibiotic medications that prohibited alcohol. The conversation was brisk and animated.

Ray realized, that for the first time since Bert was on the scene, Elsie seemed relaxed. Stan had accepted the story and the fear of discovery was gone.

After breakfast, everyone wandered into the den. Patrick was interested in Ray's gardening plans, so they went outside, carrying on an intense conversation.

"I'm not familiar with most of the plants you grow here. Sacramento is cooler than southern California, but we tend to grow most of the same things. Of course, bougainvillea is prominent throughout the state."

"It does not survive here due to the harsh winter weather. Bulbs and hardy specimens can, though, and I'm introducing more each year. Hostas are great for filling in, and provide a show all summer and well into the late fall."

"Ann mentioned a close friend. Can't remember her name but I understand she might drop by this morning?"

"Yep. Brenda. They've been close friends since high school."

The front door closed with a bang letting in the cool air of a brisk May morning. Brenda burst into the den with a big smile on her face. She walked over to Bert and as he reached for her hand, she grabbed him in a big embrace. "You have no idea how much I love you for what you just did. You saved my best friend's life."

Trailing behind her, Dan, wearing freshly pressed khakis and a beige muscle shirt, slowly approached Bert.

Bert took one look at Dan, then with a disapproving look turned to Brenda. Her face rapidly coloured and she looked away. Bert quickly turned and left. Nobody else seemed to have noticed the awkward exchange between them. Brenda tore after Bert.

He spun around. "Is it a ménage à trois or are you cheating on your best friend?" He was so angry that his fist shot up as if to hit her.

"It's not what you think. Please give me a minute to explain. Ann, Ray, Elsie and Stan have no idea what you just figured out. Please let me explain." Brenda was pleading with tears flooding her eyes. She reached for Bert's arm and he shrugged her away.

"I'm not sure there can possibly be an explanation. How can there be?"

"Let's walk." Brenda wiped her eyes with the corner of her shirt and stepped forward, straightening her back and looking Bert directly in the eyes. "It was two days before their wedding. Elsie had taken Ann to a spa in Chelsea for a mother-daughter special pre-wedding day. They were to be pampered all day and wined and dined before bed."

"That doesn't explain anything. Dan is obviously Ray's son. For God's sake, he's the spitting image of Ray. How come no one else sees it?"

Brenda moved in front of Bert and stopped him with her hand on his chest. She looked directly into his face. "Stop! Let me tell you the story."

Chapter 23

"When Elsie and Ann were about to leave for Chelsea, a picturesque village across the river in Quebec, Ann asked Ray to drop off a box of wedding decorations to me. Since our families are so small, the wedding guests only consisted of twenty-five people. It was a simple affair, and I was to decorate the dinner tables. Ray brought the box of decorations over late in the afternoon and I had invited him for dinner, which by the way, was not unusual. I greeted him at the door, holding a glass of wine. Of course, I invited him to join me for a glass. In fact, he presented me with another bottle. We had one drink, then another, then another. We rehashed wonderful memories that we shared of him and Ann, me and Ann and the three of us together. We laughed and drank. Frankly, we got roaring drunk and one thing led to another. Why, I cannot say, but the sex was more about sharing than passion. When we realized what had transpired, I'm telling you, we sobered up quickly and promised each other never to tell a soul. We never have."

Bert was listening without interrupting. The only motion he took was to pull a tissue out of a packet he had in the pocket of his navy pants. He wiped his forehead and handed Brenda a tissue, too.

"Several weeks later, I realized I was pregnant. I was terrified. I didn't know what to do. Abortion was not an option I could consider. I had betrayed my best friend and was in deep trouble. I did not have a clue how I was going to deal with this dilemma. Once I weighed my options, I booked a holiday to Mexico. When I returned, I shared with Ann that I had had a fictitious affair with a man I met there. I made up his characteristics to resemble Ray's without actually giving away the truth. She fell for the story. I told her I got caught up with this man because he reminded me of Ray in many physical ways, height, hair and eyes. The one exception I made was to tell her he was much younger than Ray and was British. She teased me mercilessly. When I left Mexico, I said I had no qualms about leaving him. It had simply been a holiday fling. Three weeks after my return, I told Ann I thought I was pregnant. I told her how terrified I was but also told her I would keep the baby. She and Ray supported me throughout the next seven and a half months. Dan was small so convincing them that he was premature was no problem Thank goodness he didn't weigh nine pounds. You've no idea how I agonized over that."

"But he's the spitting image of Ray."

"I know, and we have laughed many times that that fictitious father must have similar genes to Ray. Maybe a long-lost cousin. Even Stan and Elsie have never guessed."

Bert put his hands on Brenda's shoulders. "History does repeat itself, doesn't it?"

"Your secret is safe as long as you keep mine."

"Ah, blackmail!" Bert smiled and reached for Brenda's hand to shake on it. They returned to the house just as Kim and Boris pulled into the driveway.

Brenda introduced them and was surprised that Bert already knew Boris and the conversation became animated about barrel racing. Boris, as usual, was smartly dressed in crisp jeans and a plaid shirt. Kim wore a denim skirt and a tailored white shirt. Both wore cowboy boots. Bert told Brenda to go on into the house and warn the family that there were more guests. He said he wanted to ask Kim and Boris something before they went in.

Brenda nodded and turned to leave.

"Well, Boris, my old friend. Imagine finding you here. What a delight to meet the love of your life. So when can I go and see your ranch?" Bert had one arm around Boris's shoulders and was clutching Kim's hand with his other hand. He bent to give Kim's hand a kiss.

"I have to tell you, right now, I'm quite tired so will not stay long. We've had quite an intense few days. My husband, Patrick, is inside so, come. I want you to meet him."

"We don't intend staying either and I know we are to distance ourselves from Ann. We just wanted to drop by and bring fresh eggs and let her know that we are rooting for her. You are our champion. How can we ever thank you?"

"You have a horse called Rankler?"

"Yes. He's a beauty. Ann's got a thing about him even though he was not at his best when she saw him. He's come a long way since then, though. Boris has been working with him and I think he'll be one of our best quarter horses. But he's still a bit raw, mostly because he is still young. Why do you ask?" Kim eyed this aging man with salt-and-pepper hair worn long, framing a broad face with keen, sharp-brown eyes.

"Okay. Here's the thing. If the prognosis is positive, and I'm sure it will be, I want to buy Rankler for Ann."

Kim burst out laughing. "Have you any idea what that horse costs? He'll be a champion and we're asking a little over a half a million."

"Okay."

"Okay? Just like that! Like you can and will pay that amount?"

"Not a problem. There's one issue though. I want the horse to board with you and continue to be trained and entered into competitions. Ann will likely never be the rider, but she can be the owner."

"Holy shit! You aren't kidding, are you?"

"Please don't say anything. Once Ann is feeling stronger, I want to go to your ranch with her. Then as we are watching Rankler perform, I will present him to her. You good with this?"

Boris had a smile as broad as could be. "Well this visit has proved to be profitable."

The next hour was one of shared companionship. Both Bert and Ann, who chanced joining the group for a few minutes, begged everyone to leave as they were both exhausted.

Patrick led Bert away and Ann collapsed onto her bed. Brenda and Elsie tidied up before they left.

"The next few days are going to be cliff-hangers." Stan held the door for the women and Dan trailed behind with his mouth full of a lemon square and another clutched in his hand.

***

The following morning, Ann's checkup showed no change. This was to be expected since the transplant had really not had time to produce results.

Each day, the hours dragged on. Ann had a 7:00 standing appointment to check her blood levels. Again and again, there was no sign of improvement. Day after day, Ann and Ray left the hospital without speaking, harbouring glum thoughts. It rained every day, to Ann, a harbinger of bad news that did nothing to lift her spirits. April turned into May. Bert and Patrick were always waiting at the end of the driveway when they got home. It took only a shake of Ray's head to tell them that the results were not good. Elsie phoned almost as soon as they were in the house, and Brenda and Kim not long after.

"My friends and family are so supportive and I would give anything to be able to share good news for a change. Simply knowing how much each one cares is a blessing yet stressful at the same time. I do so want to give them good news." Ann started to shake and tears poured forth. "Damn. I can't stop this torrential flood."

Ray quickly strode across the kitchen and wrapped her in his arms. "It's only day four. The doctor said it could take five or six days to see any results. Chin up, old gal. You're too much of a trooper to let this get you down."

Bert, who had followed them into the house, handed Ann a tissue to wipe her nose on. He found a weak smile.

"Yes, I know I'm being a wimp. My resistance is low and when I'm tired my eyes leak. You boys behave while I go and take a nap."

Chapter 24

Bert and Patrick took their leave, stating that they had some business to attend to regarding doing a video for the City. They had seen a call for a proposal issued by the City for a consumer video designed to attract tourists to the area. Patrick had prepared a submission. Putting their thoughts on a work-related issue would help put their concerns for Ann aside. If this contract for Ottawa was decided in their favour, Bert would be in Canada for at least a month. Consumer-based film, intended to draw tourists to this beautiful city, was what Amazing Video was noted for. The proposal Bert and Patrick presented suggested showing the waterways, the markets, the hiking trails, shopping opportunities and how welcoming the atmosphere was. There was one very big problem, though: due to the Coronavirus, the best sites were locked down. Both Bert and Patrick hoped the restrictions would be lifted soon.

As they were heading for the mayor's office, Bert's phone rang.

"Can we meet at Major Hill's Park instead of my office? Please wear a mask and we need to keep a distance of the recommended six feet."

Patrick dug into the glove compartment where he had stored a package of masks. "Sure. Glad I picked up these little suckers."

As they drove along Colonel By Drive, they admired the blossoms that lined the road. The water in the canal was very still and it perfectly reflected the pink of the flowering trees. As they passed Main Street, they watched the Peace Tower reach for the sky and soon the Chateau Laurier Hotel came into view. Patrick had never been to Ottawa before, so was being the consummate tourist.

"The pamphlet states that the canal was built by French and Irish immigrants and that this area had been a swamp. Many of the workers contracted malaria and all the stone houses along these streets were built at the same time by the sappers working on the canal. The fact that three rivers converge here, makes this area unique."

"Our video will have to bring the history alive as well as illuminate modern day. If we land this contract, we should shoot some footage while the blossoms are out."

"Likely have to wait a year as these are almost finished, and we won't likely get a decision for at least a month."

"You're right. And that's something we need to decide. The meeting today should give us some indications of the timelines. Right now, it's quite likely to be affected by how soon this virus is beat. Do you think we can get a feeling today as to how they feel about our proposal?"

"We can try. Due to this pandemic and travel restrictions, we'll have to hire locals and I think that's one of the issues that'll work in our favour."

"Good point. Can you watch out for a parking spot?"

"Most likely we'll have to park at the National Gallery. I sure don't want to hike up those steps from the market. They're heart-attack steep."

Patrick laughed as Bert directed him to drive to the large glass building with the mammoth spider sculpture in front. Once they were parked and had exited the garage, they strode across the street to the park where Bert noted the mayor standing with another man. Bert had checked out photographs of the mayor so he would recognize him. He reached out his hand.

"Please respect distancing." The mayor's deep voice made Bert and Patrick step back.

"So sorry. These new rules are still hard to remember. I'm Bert Hansen and allow me to introduce my partner, Patrick Kells."

"George Massey is the representative of the National Capital Commission assigned to this project. The NCC is partnering with the city on this initiative. I've done some researching to see the quality of your work. It's impressive. I'm surprised a company from Sacramento is bidding on this."

"We are both Canadian from the Toronto area but have connections to Ottawa. We simply happen to do business out of California but since Ottawa is the capital of our home country we have a vested interest. The scenery and history are so captivating we wanted to take a crack at it. We felt we could do a presentation more to the interest of the tourist since that's exactly what we would be. I can assure you, if we land this contract, we will open an office here and, of course, hire a local crew to do the filming. We consider it's important to support the area."

The mayor nodded in approval. "Tourists talking to tourists. Hmm. I hadn't thought of it that way. That puts a different spin on things. Of course, you're right. You would view the project differently than someone who is familiar with the area. In other words, what you are saying is, it takes a tourist to know a tourist."

The meeting progressed for another forty minutes as they walked along the edge of the canal behind the Chateau Laurier. They stood on the edge of the canal and looked along to Rideau River to where it joined the Ottawa River. The eight stepped locks that linked the Rideau to the Ottawa was an incredible feat of engineering.

Considerable topics were covered from how the film would be structured to attract people from all parts of the globe, to the nitty gritty methods of production, and why their budget was what it was. The mayor turned to Bert and explained that he had another meeting and would contact them shortly. The City representatives left to walk to their offices and Bert and Patrick returned to the National Gallery to collect the car.

"What do you think?" Patrick slowed to a stop as they approached St. Patrick Street. He put his hand up to shelter his eyes as he gazed over the Alexandra Bridge to Quebec.

"Do you want to take a walk to Quebec?"

Patrick gave Bert an odd look then looked where he was pointing. Without delay, the two started toward the bridge. Mid way, Patrick motioned Bert to stand in the middle of the bridge so he could take a photograph.

Bert had worn a black, turtle-neck sweater and black jeans — very much the artist appearance. Bert, on the other hand, wore a grey pinstriped suit and dark grey shirt with a silver tie. He reached for Patrick's hand, drew it to his lips and smiled. "I have a good feeling, don't you?"

"When you mentioned the tourist twist, I think you nailed it, my love. I hope the other meetings were not for the same project. But if they are, I hope they're nowhere near as good as our proposal." They crossed the bridge and turned to return to Ottawa hand in hand.

Instead of going back to their hotel, Bert suggested they drop by Brenda's office. "I'm curious how a wee bit of a girl can operate a concrete company."

"What? You were never interested in concrete before."

"I know. But somehow I think there might be a video concept

there. It's sure different from the normal."

Following the GPS, they were soon parked beside Foster's Concrete.

"What's the insignia on that SUV?" Patrick was squinting out the dusty window trying to read what was on the vehicle they had parked beside.

Bert rolled down the window and read, "It's got an Ottawa-Carleton Federal Prison logo on it. I wonder what it's doing here."

"Probably need some concrete to weigh down the prisoners they want to throw in the river." Both men were still laughing when they saw Brenda come out of the building with two men. The larger man spoke with such a loud voice that Bert and Patrick had no trouble hearing what he said.

"You have to know that I'm pleased at how Jorge has settled in. I am sure he's grateful for your assistance." The large man reached for Brenda's hand then for the hand of the man nodding his head. With a wave, he walked over to the SUV, got in and drove off.

Bert watched this with interest, got out of the car and followed Brenda and this Jorge person into the office. Patrick was close on his heels. Jorge continued out to the yard and Brenda turned to greet Bert and Patrick.

"What brings you here?"

"After we spoke the other day, I wanted to see how such a little slip of a gal ran a business that most would consider a man's job." Bert wandered over to look out the back window as he spoke. "Any chance of a tour?"

"Normally, we can't go out into the yard without a hard hat and steel-toed boots, but you are lucky that it's the end of the day and all is quiet. Yes. I'd be happy to show you around. It's a good thing it's finally a clear day."

As they toured the yard, Brenda answered numerous questions about the operation. Having learned that Brenda inherited it when her father died, both men were full of admiration. The staff were leaving and as they said their goodbyes, Brenda bid each a goodnight by name. As she was explaining the concrete dumper, Dan arrived, gave his mother a quick peck on the forehead and turned to shake Bert's hand.

Dan then reached for Patrick's hand. "What's up?"

"We're nosy guys, so I wanted to see where and how your mother did business. My boy, she's one amazing woman."

"Dan, can you see if the men have left and if so, lock the front door?" Brenda was embarrassed at the compliment.

Dan turned to do as his mother asked. All three watched him stride away looking like a typical teen in scuffed runners partially covered by ragged-edged faded blue jeans. He hiked his Ottawa Senator's hockey team jacket that had slipped off his shoulder back to where it belonged. Bert noted the pride on Brenda's face.

"You did one great job with that young man. In fact, if I'm not mistaken, Jorge is another project you've taken on."

"How is it that you can read me so well?"

"A little bit of eavesdropping and putting two and two together. How long was he in prison?"

"Fifteen years,"

"Fifteen years! What did he do? Murder someone?" Bert's tone was between one of disbelief and one of being stunned.

"Yes."

Bert and Patrick stopped in their stride. "You mean — as simple as that — you hired a murderer? I'm assuming he served his time and was recently released and is on parole. Does that explain the man I overheard out front?"

"This is really none of your business, but since you asked, Ann was the one who insisted I hire Jorge."

"Ann! Now I'm really confused. Why don't Patrick and I treat you and Dan to dinner and you can fill me in on the details. And I'll tell you why I'm asking all these questions."

Dan had just sidled up to the three and overheard the dinner invitation. "Can we do Italian? The province has opened up patio dining so Luigi can set us up outside."

So it was decided that Luigi's it was. Brenda shed her coveralls and steel-toed boots and emerged looking fresh in a pair of soft-blue slacks and filmy, flowered blouse. She had pulled her deep-ash-blonde hair out of the bun and had run a brush through it. It now floated around her shoulders. She tripped down the steps in white sandals.

"My dear, I am still in awe how such a very feminine little lady can handle a crew of tough labourers and manage a large construction firm." He was admiring her as she came down the office steps.

Brenda and Dan led the way in Brenda's car and they were soon at Luigi's.

Luigi ran out from behind the counter and wrapped Brenda in his arms in a big hug. "How's my favourite gal tonight and who have you brought me?"

Brenda introduced Bert and Patrick, making sure to identify that they were from Sacramento. "But Luigi, you have to stop hugging everyone. We're in a pandemic and you don't want to be responsible for spreading the virus."

"Oh, I know. I'm so bad. But how can I not hug you?" He was

ushering them to a table outside. The yard was awash in apple blossoms. "This is my new patio. I had to be responsive to the pandemic restrictions. At least the kitchen is considered essential, so we can cook."

"Luigi was wise to put the kitchen on the other side next to the neighbouring business. He wanted to create a beautiful scene for his customers. He sure did that. Now the patio adds another delightful space to enjoy his wonderful food."

A couple of bottles of wine later — and full stomachs — the foursome were steadfast friends.

"Patrick and I have been toying with the idea of doing a documentary based on stories of strong women. What do you think, Dan? Isn't your mother one strong woman?"

"The strongest."

"Brenda, your story is definitely one we would like to consider. By the way, you did not clarify why it was Ann who introduced you to Jorge."

Brenda explained Ann's involvement. "Of course, due to the pandemic eliminating her role at the prison, and the health issues she's dealing with, it's unlikely she'll return for quite some time."

"Another strong woman. Between you, Ann and Kim, I have three likely stories right here."

Chapter 25

Ann was still resting but awake when her phone vibrated. Clearing her throat, she answered.

"Ann, it's Warden Styles. I know this pandemic has prevented you from coming to the prison, but I hope you are keeping well and safe." His gravely voice was loud and Ann held the phone away from her ear. She had not informed the prison of her health problem as the pandemic restrictions were enforced about the same time, so she did not feel it was necessary.

"I miss going there."

"Your work was such a benefit for the inmates. I do hope the lockdown is soon lifted. I have a small favour to ask in the meantime. The last time you were here, you worked with Bella and gave her one of your books to read. Honestly, Ann, this is the first time she has responded in a positive way to anything we have introduced. She asked if she can get another of your books."

"That's no problem. You can order them on line. I'll email the link."

"There's another thing. Since she responded so positively, I wondered if there is any way you can work with her remotely. Through Skype, Zoom or some other way?"

Ann was now sitting on the side of the bed. Her first thought was to turn down the suggestion. She paused. "Can I think it over? There would certainly be logistics I would have to consider, but consider them I will."

"Great. Let me know what you decide. Take care and stay safe." Ann smiled at her phone. This was the new "sign off" everyone was using.

"Ray," Ann called loudly. "Can you come here?"

Wearing a big smile and little else, Ray emerged from the bathroom where he had been showering.

"Oooh, my handsome knave, I just might have to get back under the covers."

"Now that's an invitation if ever I heard one. You sound very happy with yourself."

"I am. I've decided that I have let this disease rule me and it's not going to anymore. Each minute of each day is precious, and I intend to live it to the fullest even if my time is limited."

"Don't say that." Ray had slipped under the covers and was running his hand up Ann's back.

"We have to face facts. I could die from this damn leukemia or I could get run over by a bus, but I refuse to feel sorry for myself. I just got a call from Warden Styles and he gave me an idea of how I can still work with the prisoners. I'm halfway through a novel and I need to finish it. I have a wonderful husband who needs to get back to work and so do I. Ray, we need to move forward."

"Can you move forward with your clothes off?" Ray was obviously ready for action.

Their passion was gentle until it built to a fervour. Afterward, they lay in a comfortable embrace with Snuggles purring on the pillow beside them.

Ann filled Ray in on what her thoughts were regarding providing online instruction. The rest of the day was filled by menial chores and when they went to bed that evening, they made tender love again and fell into a deep sleep.

Day four was like the other days: no change in Ann's bloodwork.

"Well I haven't got time to fret over that, have I?"

Ray turned his head away from watching the road and looked at Ann with his eyebrows furrowed. "Okay. If you say so. What's up?"

"I need to make an appointment with a social-media guru. At least someone knowledgeable about interacting through social media. I need someone to work with me to develop those online courses for my prison friends."

"Honey, I don't want you to wear yourself out for a bunch of inmates."

"Ray! I've never heard you speak that way before. I always thought you were supportive of my volunteer work."

"I am. It's because of your health. To me you are more important than anyone, felon or not. I can't bear to take a chance on you overdoing it."

"Okay, Fly Boy. You listen to me. This whole idea has energized me. It's the first time I've felt alive since the diagnosis. Well, maybe that day at Kim's was the exception. I still can't get over Bert knowing Boris."

"Okay, Ann. You win. But promise me that if you're in the least bit tired, you'll rest and pace yourself accordingly."

Ann leaned across to the driver's seat to kiss Ray's cheek. "I promise."

As usual, Bert and Patrick were waiting at the end of the driveway and Stan pulled up as Ann and Ray arrived. Elsie stepped out of the passenger side, carrying a container box.

Patrick got out of the rental car with a huge grin on his face, leaned into the back of the sedan, and removed a large box. His back was to Ray so Ray could not see what Patrick lifted out, but Ann could.

"Patrick. Wherever did you find those?"

Patrick turned and handed Ray two dozen lavender plants. The grin on Ray's face was all the thanks he needed. The two men headed for the garden while the other four set out to make coffee and serve the cinnamon buns Elsie had made, and that still smelled as if they were fresh from the oven.

"Mom, you are spoiling me and all my friends."

At that moment, Brenda and Dan arrived. "Oh my god, is that cinnamon buns I smell?"

Before Elsie could answer, Dan was already pulling them apart. He picked up a knife and slathered one with butter. "I'm in heaven!"

"At least use a plate and try to show some of the manners I've tried and tried to drill into you." Brenda was handing Dan a plate and a serviette. "This kid is one big hollow tube. Unfillable."

Everyone laughed.

Bert was watching the scene in the kitchen while sitting at the table. He was still not quite comfortable with mingling like a family member. He watched his daughter, and crossed his fingers. He had found a new life and even though they lived across a continent, he knew the miles would not diminish what they had found together, regardless of Ann's health. He lifted his eyes to the ceiling and uttered a silent prayer: "Please, God. Save this wonderful woman."

Patrick and Ray came in the back through the laundry room and Patrick noticed Bert's concentration. He leaned over and whispered to Bert. "She is one special gift. No matter what the future holds, you have to be grateful for finding her. She has your smile, so I love her too." Bert pulled Patrick to him and gave him a kiss.

"Okay, folks. Before I hit the sack, I want to tell you what I'm going to do." Ann filled them in on the social media courses she was going to compose and deliver.

"Hey, Ann. I can help. I know all about that kind of thing." Dan spoke with his mouth full, swallowed and swigged back half a glass of milk.

"Of course, you do. I forgot that you were so up on the latest technology."

"Not just me. Li is a whiz. I'll talk to her, and tomorrow afternoon, we can brainstorm ideas." Dan picked up another cinnamon roll.

Elsie grinned. Seeing them getting eaten was all the appreciation she needed.

Dan walked over to her, towering over her, he gave her a hug and patted her bottom. "Awesome buns!"

Everyone agreed at the dual compliment. Ann excused herself to get her rest.

"Patrick and I bid on a video project for the City." Bert stood and picked up a plate, loaded it with a buttered bun, poured a coffee and watched for reaction.

"How can the City hire an American company? No offence, but we take pride in supporting our own." Stan moved beside Bert.

"We understand it might be an issue, so we made it clear that if we do get this contract, there's a possibility of opening an office here. Not sure yet, but maybe."

"I did look at some of your work on line. I sure like what you do."

"Thanks, Stan. That means a lot."

Elsie watched Stan to see if there was any suspicion of their indiscretion. Stan was patting Bert on the back like an old buddy. There was certainly no sign of any problem.

"Come and see what Patrick brought me."

Stan, Patrick, Brenda, Dan and Ann followed Ray out to the back yard. Elsie started after them, but Bert placed his hand on her arm and indicated that he wanted her to stay.

"I wanted to talk to you. First let me say, you and Stan have raised one beautiful woman and she has stolen my heart."

"Thanks, Bert. That's important to me."

"Before the rest get back, I want you to know that Patrick and I have discussed leaving our inheritance to Ann."

Elsie was about to object, but Bert held up his hand to indicate that she be quiet. "No. Don't stop me. We have no one else that we want to name in our wills. Mind you, we don't intend to pop off any time soon, but there you have it. In the meantime, we want to be a part of her life."

Elsie looked Bert square in the face, nose to nose. "Perfect! I think it's perfect. I sure know how to pick my men!"

The back door slammed shut and conversation was lively. "Ray's garden is promising to be outstanding."

An hour later, Ray shooed everyone out and insisted Ann rest.

Dan and Li arrived by bike mid-afternoon.

"Dan. Didn't the doctor tell you, no biking?"

"Like I can't manage with one hand going slowly on back streets? Honestly, Ann. It feels good to be mobile again. And I promise to be extra careful."

"Dan told me about your project. I think it's brilliant. Even without the lockdown, I think you are onto something." Li stood, coming almost up to Dan's chin, looking the picture of Asian beauty. Her long, black hair caught the light and sparked with blue highlights, and her deep skin tone was radiant. She was dressed in casual knee-length pants with a hooded navy sweatshirt.

For the next two hours, the three brainstormed. Ann and Li took notes. The air was energized, and ideas flew back and forth like spinning kites.

"Ann, I know you prefer working with your inmates on a one-on-one basis, but in developing this, we could expand the lessons and do a generalized form that could be Zoomed to prisons around the word."

"For God's sake, Dan. Don't be silly. I simply want to continue to help the inmates I've been working with."

"Dan's right." Li swept a hank of her black glossy hair off her face and leaned over toward Ann. "I don't think you realize what you have to offer. I went on line last night and tried to source courses available for prisoners. There were some general ESL courses, but they didn't even come close to what you offer. Think about it, Ann. You have an opportunity to make a huge difference."

"Okay. But while I think about it, I have to excuse myself and get some rest before I fall over." Ann carefully stood and once she had her balance, went to her bedroom.

Dan and Li packed up and left.

Ray returned with bags of groceries and a case of beer. He noted the quiet of the house, so took Snuggles out to the yard and both of them played in the dirt. A half hour later, Ann snuck up behind Ray, but Snuggles had already met her at the back steps.

"Hey, Fly Boy. You hungry?"

"Famished. Did you have a good rest?"

Over dinner, Ann told Ray about the session with Dan and Li. "The way the kids spoke, it's quite likely I may be able to extend my teaching to a broader audience. This is a little daunting but somewhat exciting, don't you think?"

"That's brilliant. Of course, you can do it. As long as you pace yourself and don't overdo it."

"Well the way Dan described setting it up, it could be a legacy I could leave."

"Jesus, Ann! Don't go there."

"Well, leukemia or not, it's a thought."

The next morning's appointment revealed nothing had changed. Ann did tell the doctor that she felt stronger, but it was likely due to the adrenalin rush from her new project.

When they got home, Bert and Patrick were not there but phoned almost immediately.

"We felt we had to take a look at possible video opportunities. We haven't heard from the City yet, but just in case …"

Ann gave Bert the news that the bone marrow transfer had not made a difference. Both were disappointed.

"Ann, I want to talk to you about another project Patrick and I have been mulling over. We'll come by in an hour or so."

"That guy's creative juices are flowing again. I can feel it." Ray had changed into grey sweatpants and a washed-to-faded brown shirt. He was headed for the garden with Snuggles close at his heels.

Ann settled into the recliner, smoothed the fabric protectors over the off-white chair, opened the book she was reading, and relaxed.

Chapter 26

Bert's hello echoed though the house when he and Patrick arrived. Ann started to rise from the chair.

"No. Stay where you are."

Ann nodded and settled back. Bert and Patrick sat on the sofa opposite Ann and leaned forward to capture Ann's attention.

"Bert has an idea and we want to run it by you."

"This visit, and the wonderful people we've met, has given me an idea for a documentary. We are ecstatic about the concept. I think it has certain merit. Sometimes, we like to undertake a project for its artistic merit instead of always doing money-generating films."

Ann watched this man who was her biological father. For the first time, she felt a connection. He was creative and so was she. His creativity energized him. Hers did too.

"We are considering doing a film featuring strong women in non-traditional roles."

Bert settled back onto the cushions. Patrick still leaned forward.

"What do you think?"

"It's quite interesting. It depends on what you mean and how you would present it."

"Brenda is a prime example. Not only does she run an impressive male-dominated business, she single-handedly has raised a great son. My thinking is to present vignettes showing women working in unusual circumstances, ones that the general public think of as being male bastions."

Ray came in and overheard the tail end of the conversation.

"Men seldom realize what women do."

"Well Brenda can certainly tell you some hilarious stories about being accepted in that role. I have watched her straighten up to her full five feet and talk down to big burly men. And you know something? They nearly always end up listening to her, admiring her. Yes she is an excellent example."

"And so are you." Ray stood in stocking feet after shedding his boots when he came into the house. He moved beside Ann.

"Well, thank you. You're a little biased, I think. There are tons of women out there who write novels, memoirs and are journalists. Well, maybe featuring a journalist in a war-torn country would qualify. My work is definitely not thought of as a male-dominated world."

"No, honey. I'm not talking about your writing. Bert, did you know she works with prisoners?"

"Brenda told me. And I've met Jorge. Anyway, we are pursuing this idea and Patrick has to return to the office and nose about to see if there are any investors interested in this idea. We might fund it ourselves, but first, we will try to find a sponsor. At this point, it's simply an idea to pursue."

"Tell Bert and Patrick about *your* new idea."

Ann's phone buzzed and she answered to tell her mother that there had been no new news. When she ended the call, she told Bert and Patrick about the video-conferencing idea.

"We can certainly help with that, my dear."

Day five went the same as the others: no change. Ann left the cancer clinic with her head low and her eyes staring at the lines in the pavement.

"That sweet man came all the way from California with expectations of making me well. Each day that passes pushes that further from a possibility."

"The days are still within the range of being on target. You must not get depressed. Think positive. Remember. You told me to kick your butt if you got to feeling sorry for yourself. Well, my dear. Bend over."

"Okay, okay, Ray. I get it. But each morning we come here, I have my fingers crossed and each morning has been a letdown. Right now, I wish I could have a great big glass of wine."

"That too, is not going to happen. Let's go and see if Bert and Patrick are around."

Bert had seen Patrick off on a plane heading for Santiago. When Ray and Ann caught up with Bert, his mood matched Ann's.

"This is not doing either of you any good. Let's see if we can make the afternoon better."

"Dan and Li are coming over this morning to go over some details of doing video conferencing. I expect it may go well into the afternoon, then I'll have to rest." Ann gave Bert a hug. "I know you will be lonely without Patrick, but how about a barbeque this evening?"

The three parted company with the promise to be more cheerful when they checked in for dinner. Ann called her mother and father to invite them to join them.

Before Dan and Li arrived, Ann called the warden and told him what she was planning. He asked her to put together a proposal and instead of her volunteering, this might be something the board would subscribe to, and she might be paid for her services.

"Well, Warden. Your facility will be my testing ground so let's continue to do it on a volunteer basis with only the inmates I have worked with to date. If it *is* a success, then I can put together a proposal or proposals. I intend to do a Zoom class for multiple people and one to work one-on-one. This is new to me, too, so let's see how it goes. I sent along the link for my book. Did you get it?"

"I ordered and received it, thanks. Bella is already well into it. I hope you can work virtually with her soon. She might be the ideal one for you to start with as she's quite intelligent. She still has a number of years before her sentence is finished, but in the meantime, this might be a way to break down the anger and make her feel worthwhile. Prison is more than a place to confine criminals, it's also meant to provide rehabilitation. Bella has some potential to be able to adjust in society. I do wish she could lose some weight, though."

"I agree. She is the perfect choice. I think I may have something ready by next week. I'll let you know."

Ann disconnected, set her phone on the end table, stood, moved away from her desk, then turned to Ray.

"Well?"

"He was very receptive. This project is exactly what I need. It's not physically demanding and it helps to be working on something that takes my mind off that dreaded word leukemia."

"Patrick should be landing soon. I wonder how Bert will manage without him and him without Bert. You know, they make an amazing couple. Sometimes Patrick finishes Bert's sentences, just like any old married —"

"Sometimes that's a good thing but, my Fly Boy, be careful you don't read my thoughts too closely."

"Oh yeah. Off with your clothes, woman."

"Stop it! Your mind reading is centred on the nether regions.

Not now. The kids are on their way over. I hope to accomplish at least some small segment of what to do as a lesson plan. You can go play outside with Snuggles."

Ray slid his hand down the side of Ann's cheek, ran it around her throat, pulled her to him and gave her a deep, passionate kiss. Rebuffed again, he called the kitten and headed for the garden. Snuggles followed close at his heels all the way to the back yard and Ann went to her office.

"Darn, Snuggles. I need my girl to get better. This is too difficult."

The kitten drifted around Ray's ankles, purring away, happy to be spoken to, not caring what the topic was.

Dan and Li arrived and settled in right away to show Ann how to set up Zoom as an instructional site and showed her how to remain visible while she did a PowerPoint presentation.

"That's totally amazing. I can't believe how easy it is. I may give it a test run in a day or two with a female prisoner the warden is anxious for me to work with. Fingers crossed it'll be successful. You have shown me so much this session. You kids are amazing!"

"Hey. Glad to help. Now what's for lunch?"

Ann laughed at Dan and gave him a swat on the shoulder. "There's no way that hollow leg of yours will ever get filled. Come on. I think Ray finished in the garden and has rustled up some lunch."

As soon as they got to the kitchen, Dan and Li sat on the floor and played with Snuggles. Dan panned the laser beam along the floor and up the wall. Snuggles went berserk trying to catch it. Everyone laughed at his antics.

"You know, this is exactly what I needed. I was feeling so

sorry for myself. Now I feel grateful to have such wonderful people on my team, not to mention a crazy cat. Come. Let's eat."

Dan and Li left right after lunch and Ann headed for her afternoon nap. Before she drifted off, she thought about how the past few weeks had impacted her family and friends.

Everyone's nerves were stretched to the breaking point. Elsie was baking every day simply to try to keep her mind off events. She had her freezer full of muffins, dozens of cookies packed away, and was in the process of making cheese bread which she planned to bring to the evening barbeque.

"Now that I've met Bert again, I can't believe it, but I'm really quite relaxed around him. Our moment of indiscretion doesn't even seem to be important. He is a lovely man." Elsie was muttering to herself.

Stan was pacing back and forth, making a path on the carpet. Every now and again he stopped, looked out the window and resumed pacing. He was nursing a headache and had a sore throat. Because he was a bit off colour, they decided to stay in for the afternoon, hoping Stan would feel better and be able to join in the fun of the barbeque.

Brenda sent numerous prayers to the heavens whenever she had a spare moment or when business slowed and the busy yard quieted enough to gave her a break. "Please, dear God, I beg you to heal my friend."

"Excuse me, ma'am, were you talking to me?" Randy had come into the office from the back entrance.

"No. Thanks, Randy, I was just talking to myself."

Brenda was glad Ann had shared the story about Bert and she was pleased to finally have someone who shared the knowledge of Dan's parentage. She trusted Bert to be discrete and keep their secrets. Ann had called and invited her to join them for the evening, so when she finished work, she ordered a pizza for Dan and drove over to Ann and Ray's.

The news of Ann's new venture got everyone offering bits and pieces of advice. Brenda suggested that the inmates learn how to fill out forms. She noted that this was one difficulty that Jorge had when he started working for her.

"They need to know how to apply for a job, complete an application for health insurance, and register for a driver's license."

"Brenda, that's brilliant!"

Stan was feeling better, and he and Elsie arrived with lots of baked goods. He nodded and added that getting a credit card was easy, but they needed to read the small print.

"No, Dad. I think that's something they do learn. Most inmates are pretty savvy when it comes to street smarts."

Right after supper, Stan excused himself, begging off with a headache, so he and Elsie left. Stan had eaten little and was anxious to leave. Everyone decided to go home early, always aware that Ann needed her rest, and they knew she had an early appointment at the clinic.

Elsie gave her daughter a long hug and whispered in her ear that she hoped the next day would be rewarding.

"Well, folks. Day six tomorrow. Let's hope!" Ray was ushering everyone out the door.

"Let's hope," came back as a chorus.

Chapter 27

In the morning, Ray and Ann drove, once again, to the cancer clinic. The route was so familiar now, and they drove in silence, each with the same silent thoughts, thoughts of hope.

As always, Ann was taken into one of the labs and Ray waited in the lounge. When Ann appeared, looking desolate, she told Ray that the doctor wanted to see them both together.

"This is not a good sign." Ray took Ann's hand.

Their eyes met. The love they shared gave them comfort and prepared them for what the doctor might have to say.

Once the nurse deposited them in the doctor's office, they continued to hold onto each other but avoided eye contact.

As was his habit, the doctor arrived, closed the door quietly behind him and sat in his chair. He swept the wayward crop of blond hair off his forehead and leaned forward. "We have some positive readings this morning."

Ann and Ray looked up, their eyes wide open; their mouths half-open.

"Does that mean the bone marrow transplant worked?"

"It appears so." Dr. Helms was grinning. He reached for their hands that were still clasped. "I think it worked. I'm certain it worked. Now we should see improvement day by day. But keep in mind that your immune system is still fragile and you still need to be cautious. You will find that you will get stronger each day and might be tempted to overdo it. Please don't. You need to know that your system has been compromised. To fully return to normal, could take a year or more."

Neither Ann nor Ray spoke. Tears rolled down their cheeks

and Dr. Helms handed then each a tissue.

He stood up and left. He knew that Ray and Ann needed a few moments on their own. When he returned, it was to smiling faces. Instead of the usual handshake when they said their goodbyes, Ray grabbed the doctor and gave him a big hug. Ann did the same.

When they were in the car, Ray started to shake. "I'm not sure I can drive right now. You have no idea how much this has affected me."

"Of course I do. Listen, Fly Boy. Pull yourself together and let's get our people together to celebrate."

Elsie ran into the house. "Are they sure? I'm beside myself with excitement. Come here, dear."

Clasped together, they felt the special bond between mother and daughter.

Stan stayed at home, nursing what he thought was a cold, but was on the phone.

Bert arrived in a flurry and raced into the kitchen. "Oh, my dear people. Our prayers have been answered."

Stan yelled over the phone to Bert. "You save my daughter's life. There's no reward big enough to thank you."

Bert beamed. He had his reward. In fact, he had two: one, he had found his daughter, and two, his bone marrow was saving her life. "Excuse me. I have to phone Patrick." He went out to the front lawn to make the call as the reception was better there.

Brenda breezed past him.

The front door slammed and Brenda appeared in the kitchen doorway, her face flushed and with hands clasped to her heart. She slowly approached her dearest friend, tenderly touched her cheek then wrapped her arms around her to give her a bear hug.

Dan was steps behind her and nodded in agreement.

Stan started to cough into the phone.

"What's wrong with Dad?"

"Oh, he must have picked up a nasty bug. He can't seem to shake it."

"For God's sake, Elsie. Get him tested for Covid-19. This pandemic is spreading quickly and it's a very dangerous bug."

"Oh, I don't think that's what it is. He just has a cold."

"Regardless, Mom. You need to insist that he get tested. If he's positive, all of us might have been exposed. Please go right now. Make sure he goes to a test site."

Reluctantly, Elsie left with the promise to get Stan to a Covid-19 test site. Ray had checked on line and there was one at a convenient location. When she told Stan, he was about to refuse but decided to err on the side of caution because of Ann.

The wait at the test centre was only a few minutes and a swab was taken from his nose. He was told to isolate, regardless, and he would have results within twenty-four hours. The technician insisted that Elsie be tested at the same time.

When they got home, Stan was really tired and went to bed for a nap. Elsie phoned Ann.

"Well that was not pleasant. We didn't even have to get out of the car, though. The testing person comes right to you to do the swab. To do the test, they stick the swab up your nose and push it into your brain, I swear. Anyway, we have to stay isolated until we know the results. That should be tomorrow. Your dad is tired so has gone to bed. I downloaded a novel so will settle in the recliner and read it."

"Nasty business, but I'm glad you took my advice. You know I can't be exposed to anything and have to be really careful for at least a year."

Stan was still feeling tired the next morning and was running a fever. Shortly after lunch, which neither of them ate very much of, the phone rang.

"Mrs. Rider. This is the lab. I'm afraid your husband has tested positive for the Coronavirus. You were negative. Please phone your doctor for instructions and do not go near your husband. He will need to isolate for ten days. Will you be able to do that?"

"He can stay in the bedroom. Will that work?"

"Please stay as far away from him as possible and wipe down everything he has touched with a disinfectant. You will need to take another test in four days. Has anyone else been exposed to your husband? If so, they need to go to the nearest test site and get tested."

Elsie hung up the phone and called the doctor right away.

"Mrs. Rider. Please be very careful. If Stan shows any signs of having difficulty breathing, get him to a hospital immediately. Infected people can have a mild dose or suffer serious symptoms." The doctor explained the severity of the infection and what Elsie was to do and how she was also to isolate even though she tested negative.

"But I have to go shopping."

"I'm sorry, but you must isolate. All stores are delivering. I will have the drug store send over some prescriptions for Stan. They will ring the bell and place the order at the door then move away."

Ann's phone rang and she saw it was her mother. "Sweetheart, Dad tested positive. Everyone needs to get tested. Oh, I do hope everyone's all right. You especially. We are confined to the house until your father is no longer contagious."

"We went through this with Ray, so I know what you have to do. We'll get the tests to be on the safe side. Let me know what you need for groceries or medications and we'll drop them off. Of course, we will leave them on the porch. I pray Dad is okay and has a mild dose. This is a very dangerous virus and people are dying from it. Both of you, please take care of yourselves. Love you."

When Ann ended the call, she told Ray about the conversation. She then called Bert and Brenda and insisted they get tested. Without delay, she and Ray went to the nearest test centre. Fortunately, everyone's tests came back negative but because they had been exposed to Stan, they all had to be retested within four days but needed to isolate in the meantime. Four days later, they got the all-clear, much to everyone's relief. Bert had alerted Patrick to get tested too.

Stan, other than being very tired, was lucky that he had a mild case. His temperature returned to normal within two days, and he and Elsie spent their time reading, playing cards and watching movies. Elsie still tested negative after two tests.

They realized how fortunate they had been when one of Stan's friends was hospitalized and had to be put on a ventilator. He may have been the source of where Stan contacted the virus, but they would not likely ever know for sure. His friend fought for his life for weeks and was finally able to breathe on his own. He would remain in the hospital for an indefinite length of time. He was not able to have visitors and even if he were near death, his family could not see him. Learning this made Elsie and Stan thankful that they were able to resume a normal life after two weeks.

"Not only did we narrowly miss being very sick, but we could have exposed Ann and that could have been fatal. I shudder to think of the consequences." Elsie was folding the laundry. The sheets and towels had to be laundered every day.

"Perhaps all the medications Ann is taking held the virus at bay."

"Regardless, we got off easy. I'm going to make lasagna and celebrate that we can be together again. There's a restriction that family and friends are to only see certain people. It's actually a contact number of ten in what they are calling their 'bubble' group."

"Even with that, because Ann is still vulnerable, we have to socialize outside. We can't take any chances."

Three hours later, Elsie bundled up the lasagna and she and Stan headed for the car.

Ray had the fire pit roaring and the entire bubble group consisting of Brenda, Dan, Li, Bert, Kim, Boris, Elsie, Stan, Ray and Ann were there to celebrate Ann's continuing progress and Stan's recovery.

Chapter 28

Ann did progress at a steady pace. The chemo had caused some hair loss, but it had stopped, so Ann had it cut to a close-cropped helmet. There were a few grey strands, but she rather liked them. She insisted she needed to walk every day, not only for the exercise, but for her mental health. Jason accompanied her several times a week, being careful to observe social distancing.

"So how is that wee kitten doing?"

"Wee is no longer applicable. He is a darling. Life at the Rogers household is definitely much more interesting, and he rules. Jason, he is the best thing to come into our lives. No. I think Bert ranks number one. But Snuggles is the lord of the house. Ray spoils him and Snuggles rewards him by purring so loud you would think we had a lion in the house."

Jason laughed. "So you called him Snuggles? I like it."

Ann was pleased to walk with Jason and hear about him and Walter. Jason was surprised that Bert was married to Patrick, and was delighted. He was knowing and understanding same-sex relationships.

Ann always felt energized when she returned from walking. Now that she was feeling so much better, she worked on the project for the prison inmates. She advanced the novel, and her agent was pleased. Ray was scheduling short flights. He requested that he be given day trips so he could be home for the night, and found he was happy to be piloting a plane again. Life was starting to resume a somewhat normal pattern by mid-summer.

Bert was meeting on several occasions with City

representatives trying to convince them that Amazing Video be contracted to do the tourism film. He suggested that it be a series of segments to be released strategically, to keep the potential target engaged. As he was leaving yet another meeting, his phone vibrated. He leaned against the rental BMW.

"Hey, Patrick, my love. How are you doing?"

"Are you sitting down?"

"I'm leaning against the fender of the car on a glorious day here in Ottawa."

"You were right on the button! The idea you have for the strong women video? Well. We have sponsorship."

"Fantastic! How many sponsors and how much are they in for?"

"No, Bert. That's why I asked if you were sitting. We have one sponsor."

"Oh. Okay. That's a start. How much?"

"You'd better hang onto something."

"What is it you're saying?"

"We only have one sponsor because they want to be exclusive. They will fund the entire project!"

"What?"

"That's what I said. *The entire project!*"

"Who is it and how did you tap into them?" Bert was now stomping about going around and around the car.

"It was one of those crazy flukes. I was at the racetrack and was talking to Harold Manchester. He asked what we were working on. While I was explaining this project, a friend of his edged closer and listened in to everything I said. I had no idea who he was and thought him a bit intrusive, but I held my tongue and answered his questions."

"And?"

"Finally, Harold realized that he had not introduced us and did so. He was the fucking CEO of Bowing."

"The steel manufacturer?"

"Yes. The steel company. Next thing I knew, he wanted the proposal in writing, stating that he had an interest in what we were thinking. He wanted it on his desk the next morning. This guy does not mess around."

"But why was he interested?"

"As it turns out, the company has a philanthropic program that promotes and sponsors females working, or intending to work, in non-traditional employment."

"Now that is what I call luck."

"I emailed the proposal, and within four hours, an email arrived asking if Bowing could have exclusivity. Until I saw his name on the bottom of the email, I didn't even know his name. It's Stephen Brown, by the way. Stephen Brown, CEO, Bowing limited."

"Un fucking believable!"

"Well, my dear …"

"Hold on. I have another call."

"Mr. Hansen. It's the mayor. Are you still in the area?"

"Actually, I'm in the parking lot."

"Please come back to my office. We have decided to offer Amazing Video the contract."

"I'm so pleased. I'll be up shortly. I'm on a call to California but will come directly."

"Patrick! I'm peeing my pants here! That was the mayor. We got the contract!"

"Stop shouting! You'll burst my eardrums. Now *I* need to sit down. Do you realize that we have just secured enough business for two years?"

The phone conversation raced back and forth between the two men who were flushed with excitement. They finally concluded the call and Bert hurried to the mayor's office.

Bert shook the mayor's hand sealing the deal with the promise of getting together to sign the agreement the following Tuesday. He left downtown and knew he needed to share his wonderful news with Ann. He got on the onramp for the 417 and headed for Stittsville.

When Bert burst into the house, Ann looked up with her mouth open. She had never seen him so excited, almost but not quite, considering how he'd reacted to the bone marrow success. His face was flushed, and his forehead was wet with sweat. He bent over with his hands on his knees and drew short breaths until he had composed himself.

"What is going on with you? Don't you dare have a heart attack when I'm starting to care so much for you."

Bert was waving one arm trying to ward her off and indicate that he was fine. "I suppose I am a little flustered but Patrick and I have so much to share. All good news." Bert slid onto a chair and put his forearms on the table, palms up.

Ray came into the kitchen, drying his hands on a towel. He had been working in the garden and had finished for the day. At Ann's signal, he sat at the table beside Bert.

"Ann. Could I have a cold glass of water please? And Ray, will you call Brenda and ask her if she can leave work and come over? It's important."

Ann handed Bert the water chilled with ice cubes. "You are not so flushed now. I thought you were on the verge of a heart attack. Whatever is going on?"

"All in due time. Ray. Phone Brenda and see if she's able to break away and come over?"

Ray ended the call. "She said Randy can take over for the rest of the afternoon. She's as curious as hell, too. What's up, Bert?"

Bert downed his drink, handed the glass to Ann indicating a refill.

Ann handed Bert the second glass of ice-water then sat in the chair across from him. She noted that he was wearing a business suit, a navy and black stripe so fine, you could hardly see the stripes. He wore a charcoal shirt and his favourite silver tie. Ann was still in sweats after her walk and Ray had on faded jeans and a white body shirt.

"I am able to tell you that we got the contract for the Ottawa tourism project. I can now tell you how it was proposed. We'll do four segments, one for each season and each segment will have at least eight activities. We suggested that we do an in-town and out, highlighting the city, the suburbs, and the valley. Apparently, the other proposals were primarily city related. The mayor and the NCC rep, George Franks, like the fact that we recognized that Ottawa was not simply a city, but was the hub for a lifestyle, and offered enticing scenery and activities — not to mention dining and entertainment. This means we'll start this winter. That means, Patrick and I will be here in Ottawa eight times over the next two years. Well. Likely more than that."

Brenda arrived and breezed in with her usual saunter, threw her shoulder bag on the counter and gave everyone a hug. "Now what is the big hullabaloo?"

Ray decided that it was time for a celebratory drink.

"Sweetheart. There's a bottle of champagne in the bar fridge."

Ray was off like a shot, returning with the bottle.

Ann, in the meantime, had produced flute glasses.

"Well I sure a hell will not refuse a glass of bubbly even though I have no idea what the occasion is."

Everyone burst out laughing and then Bert filled Brenda in on what had happened to date, while Ray filled the glasses including one for Ann.

"Hold off. I want to tell you the rest of the story. I want to get Patrick on the phone." When Patrick answered, Bert put the phone on speaker mode.

"Okay, Patrick. I want you to tell our new family what you told me a few hours ago."

The only sound in the room was Patrick's voice coming over the phone.

Ray reached for Ann's hand, then for Brenda's with his other.

Bert stood facing them, holding the phone aloft. The grin on his face and his sparkling eyes were infectious.

When Patrick had completed telling everyone what he could, there was silence for a few seconds, then shouting and clapping.

Ray held his glass high. "Here's to two amazing friends."

"No. Here's to amazing new family members." Ann gave Bert a kiss on his cheek then held him close.

Brenda held back a little, not certain how to react to the fact that her life was going to be made into a video.

Bert realized her concern and was quick to explain. "Instead of it being a video featuring numerous women, it is going to be shot as shorts. Each story will be enacted by professional actors, and other than a claim that the story is true, there will be no mention of the person it's about. That way, we can protect your identity."

Brenda relaxed and reached her glass out for a refill.

Questions and answers flew among the group with everyone wanting to know all the details.

In the midst of their celebrations, Ann's phone beeped.

"Ann, it's Kim."

"I know that, it pops up on the screen. What's up, dear friend?"

"Well, I have no idea how long Bert intends to stay here, but I wanted to know if you could bring him to the ranch."

"Your timing is perfect. Bert will only be here until next Wednesday then he has to head back to California."

"There's an international competition this weekend. Why don't you all come?"

"What a great idea! Will Rankler be competing?"

"Both afternoons. I can organize a separate canopy for your gang, and we'll make it a party to celebrate your recovery."

"My ongoing mending would be more like it, but that sounds fantastic. I am delighted to be able to show Mom and Dad as well as Brenda and Dan what you do. What time should we be there?"

"I will expect you early afternoon." Ann and Kim disconnected.

Bert excused himself, went outside and called Kim.

Chapter 29

Saturday dawned bright with a cloudless sky. In a moment of brilliance, Bert ordered a small bus to take them to the ranch.

Stan parked their car beside Ann's on her driveway and stepped out of the car, donning a Stetson hat. He was wearing a plaid shirt, jeans and cowboy boots.

"Howdy, folks."

"Dad. Wherever did you find that get-up?"

"Oh, your old man has a few things tucked away from another time. Check out your mother.

Elsie stepped out of the car and she, too, put a white Stetson on her head. She was wearing a fringed jacket, white jeans and white cowboy boots.

"Man oh man. I'm blown away. How did you come up with those clothes?"

"I think we told you often enough that your mother and I went to the Calgary Stampede. I guess we neglected to show you the outfits we purchased. They have been nicely tucked away in the storage rental. Your mother went over yesterday and brought them home. Surprisingly they still fit. Well. Almost. Just a tiny bit snug here and there."

"I love it! You are so totally into the spirit of the day."

"At least I wore jeans." Brenda was admiring Elsie's jacket. "This is retro and probably worth a penny or two today. If you ever want to sell it, Elsie, keep me in mind."

The bus arrived and they all clambered on in high spirits. Ray opened a bottle of wine and by the time they reached the ranch, it was quite a rowdy group of passengers.

"Bert. This was genius hiring the bus. This way, we don't have to worry about drinking and driving."

As they pulled into the laneway of Tall Tree Ranch, a young man directed them to a tent near the starting gate. The bus then parked in a designated area near the entrance and the driver blended into the crowd. Bert took off to find the betting booth, while the rest of the party claimed the tent area.

Kim roared into their midst.

"Hey. Welcome, everyone. We're delighted you were all able to come. Where's Bert?"

"Oh, he's off to see if he can lose lots of money today."

Kim laughed. "Before the events start, there will be a few announcements and then the show begins. I hope Bert gets back before then?"

"Why the big interest in what Bert is doing?" Ann had her arm around Kim's waist. "Did you see the outfits Mom and Dad are wearing?"

"Love them. In fact, you all look very sporting. Oh, here comes Bert." Kim strode across the grass to meet him.

They stopped for a few moments and Ann noticed they were whispering.

"It seems my friend is quite taken with Bert. I wonder what they're whispering about."

Right then, the loudspeaker squawked and the crowd went quiet. Once the feedback cleared, Boris came on the microphone to welcome the visitors. "Hosting an international event like this has been my fondest dream and here we are. Contestants have come from near and far, from across Canada and the United States. We even have one entry from Mexico. We are fortunate that the lockdown was eased and outdoor events could continue.

Please do practise social distancing and wear masks when not with your bubble group. The judges are ready as are the contestants for the first round."

He went on to list the riders and horses.

Carrying a flag, a gentleman in a suede jacket climbed onto the stand.

The first rider eased into the gate area and waited.

The flag was raised and when it was brought swiftly down, the horse started for the paddock.

Ann explained to her parents and Brenda and Dan what was happening and the rules of the sport. They were now crowding the fence and it was clear that everyone was caught up in the action.

"For some reason, we do not have programs. Dan, can you collect some for us, please."

Dan swaggered off asking for directions as he went.

"Next rider is Amy Skelton on Rankler owned by Ann Rogers."

"What? There must be a mistake."

"No, my dear friend. There is no mistake." Kim nudged Bert forward.

Bert handed Ann some documents. "Rankler is my gift to an amazing woman who enticed me from California. My admiration for her talents, her commitments, and her strengths, warrant a just reward. Ann, I knew you were smitten with Rankler so it is my pleasure to gift him to you."

"No, no, no, Bert. You can't do that. It's beyond anything I could consider."

"Shush. He's in the gate. Watch."

Rankler stood ready. He looked relaxed except his ears were

back and his eyes were watching the paddock entrance. The flag lowered and as soon as the rider gave a simple dig into his flanks, Rankler raced into the paddock. He rounded the three barrels without touching or toppling a single one. As he came around the third barrel, he leaned over so far he was almost on his side. Ann feared he would fall over but he held his balance and cleared the course.

"That's a great time. He might take this heat!" Kim was jumping up and down. "Ann. You have a winner there."

"But I can't accept him. Bert. Please. This is far too much."

"You listen, my little lady. I am a very wealthy man and I am definitely giving you this horse. Kim, Boris and I have worked everything out. Rankler will stay here and be managed by Boris. We have established an account to settle any expenses for his keep. But seeing his performance this afternoon, I expect he will generate more revenue than what his costs will be. You, my dear, have only to enjoy owning him. You have no idea how much pleasure being able to do this has given me."

"I am flabbergasted. Delighted, of course, but totally blown away. There is no way I can thank you enough."

She embraced Bert with teary eyes. "Kim. Can I go over to see Rankler now?"

"Of course, and you need to meet the rider. She's one of our staff and will likely be working with him on an ongoing basis."

Elsie rushed up beside Ann. "Oh, this is all so exciting. Imagine owning a horse and one so splendid. His coat simply glows. Can I come to meet him, too?"

As it turned out, everyone followed Ann and Kim across the grass to an area near the barn. All the horses were corralled there, and Amy was towelling Rankler, praising him all the while.

When Ann approached, she stepped back and as if he knew, Rankler snorted and lowered his head for Ann to stroke him. He nuzzled her neck as she stroked his. It was a love match.

Bert was busy taking pictures for messaging to Patrick. Brenda was also taking lots of pictures. "You know, Kim, if this is appropriate, I think your ranch and a barrel event would make a fantastic corporate outing. I would love to bring my staff here. Is that something that would be possible?"

"I think it's a great idea. I'll mention it to Boris. See if it might be something we want to promote to other companies. Actually, it's a brilliant idea and especially suited for small companies. Brenda, it's brilliant. My mind is racing with possibilities. Now let's get back to the tent and have a glass of bubbly."

The cork popping brought cheers from everyone. Kim filled glasses and uncovered an array of hors d'oeuvres.

Plates were quickly loaded up and Ray lifted his glass to propose a toast. "To my lovely wife and our newfound friend, Bert. May they continue to bring joy to our lives."

"Hear, hear," a chorus of voices joined in.

Kim strode over to Ann and gave her another hug. "I am so delighted to see you are starting to mend. That was a scary few months. You have no idea how concerned we were. I see you are sipping champagne."

"I'm actually defying doctor's orders, but this is such a special occasion, I decided to risk it. I feel like all the burdens of my illness are receding and I can look forward to moving ahead with my new projects."

"Oh? And what are you up to now, my dear."

Ann explained how she was developing an online system to continue her work with inmates at the detention centre.

"You'd better be careful or she'll have you hiring her pet prisoners." Brenda had joined her friends and heard Ann telling Kim about what she did.

"No way! Why would I ever do that? I don't even understand why Ann wants to associate with them. I understand that the ones here in Ottawa are pretty hardened criminals and many are murderers."

"That's true and I recently hired one. He is on parole, and I have to say, it's one of the best decisions I have ever made."

"He must not be a murderer then."

"He is. Was."

"Aren't you terrified that he might commit murder again?"

"At first I was very reluctant. But Ann convinced me to give it a try. She assured me he was a changed man after fifteen years behind bars. She was right. He is an exemplary employee."

"Hmm. Are there any other inmates that might be suitable for working on the ranch?"

"I just started working with a female inmate and I think she's interesting. I have no idea how long her sentence might be, but I do know it will not be finished soon. The warden has taken an interest in her and hopes she can be rehabilitated to fitting into society. You and I can discuss this further. Perhaps the warden will give her a special leave permit to work here as part of her rehabilitation. She's very bright but has a temper."

Bert approached Kim. "My dear girl. I will be leaving for California this week and won't be back until winter. Patrick and I scored a contract with the City that will bring us to Ottawa off and on over the next two years. We're also working on another project in which I can see you playing a role. We will meet again. In the meantime, I am so fortunate to have found a new family here. And what a bonus finding Boris and barrel racing. Who would have thought?"

"Isn't it funny how life has its twists and turns? Let's hope this new virus that is spreading rapidly across the world will not hamper our relationship. Take care, my friend, and stay safe."

"I have an idea. Why don't we all go to Luigi's tonight?"

"Can't do. Remember. This virus has put certain restrictions on our lives. However, I can order up all the food and we can have a backyard celebration. Stan can bring his guitar and we can give Bert a grand send-off."

It was agreed that everyone would come for 7:30 as this would give Ann time for a late afternoon nap.

Dan had been quiet all afternoon but perked up when the mention of Italian food was the topic. "Mom. Can I ask Li to join us?"

Brenda looked over at Ann and Ray for their input. "Yes, but she still must observe social distancing, especially from Ann. I know this whole virus business is a nuisance, but we have barely missed it twice now and I do not want to take chances."

Ann gave Dan a look that made him nod in agreement.

The evening was one of celebration in recognition of Ann's recovering health and sadness at losing Bert — albeit only for a few short months.

Stan played his music and everyone tried to keep rhythm by mastering the spoons.

Snuggles wandered from one to the other, demanding petting and belly rubs. He had gotten over being shy around strangers.

Ann sat quietly in their midst and recollected how the last five months had changed her life. So much had happened, it had changed everyone's life.

Summer was drawing to a close and the evenings were shorter. As the hours passed, everyone grew quiet. Each in turn embraced Bert, knowing he was leaving and not knowing when they would see him again. He would be missed.

Bert stood up and moved so everyone could see him. He blew kisses all around. "Well, my dear friends. These past few months have been incredibly full and rewarding. I treasure the newfound family and friends that will forever be in my heart. Now it is time to bid you all farewell. We will keep in touch, and we will meet again."

Title: When Secrets become Lies

- Author: Molly O'Connor
- Publisher: TotalRecall Publications, Inc.
- Paperback, ISBN: 9781590954300
- eBook, ISBN: 9781590954317

A tragic accident changed Philippa's life forever. Her parents death lead to the discovery that she may not be who she thought she was. While Philippa searches for her identity, she finds friendship and romance. A back story full of adventure takes place the year of her birth and reveals who she really is in a very surprising ending.

Title: While She Was Gone

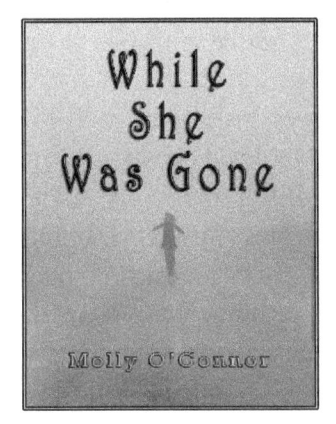

- Author: Molly O'Connor
- Publisher: TotalRecall Publications, Inc.
- Paperback, ISBN: 9781590954126
- eBook, ISBN: 9781590954133

She left a beautiful home, a handsome husband and three adorable children, and didn't return for seven years. What happened to her?

About the Author

Living in a century-old, three-generation, farmhouse in rural Ontario, Molly hovers over her laptop downing coffee after coffee while she goes on a journey with her characters. Primarily known as a writer of short stories, *When Secrets Become Lies* was her first novel, published in 2015. Previously, she published a collection of short stories, *Fourteen Cups*; a creative memoir, *Wandering Backward*; and a children's book, *Snow Business*. Her stories appear in five *Chicken Soup for the Soul* anthologies, three OIW anthologies, NYMB, magazines and newspapers. She gives writing seminars, is often a guest speaker and sings in two choirs. In her spare time, she can be found hiking the byways in Ontario and the ranges in Arizona with her camera strung around her neck, all the while thinking where her protagonist is heading next.

While She Was Gone is her second novel. An avid believer that women are limitless in the roles they choose to play, Molly places her female characters in non-traditional professions challenging the alpha male dominance factor. She also enlightens the reader about little discussed mental anxiety and depression issues. That being said, her work is about story-telling, she buries the issues in a fast-paced novel. She captures the reader right from the first page and takes them on a journey of discovery.

Contact Molly at www.mollyoconnor.ca

Acknowledgements

There are many to whom I could express heartfelt thanks that so kindly cheer me on through the process of weaving a story onto pages. You know who you are.

When writing a book an author needs to have an ear or two. Never one to shy away from lending me hers, Jessie Hunter was my constant and valued critic. Her instincts caught many an awkward moment and she knew when I needed praise.

Sherrill Wark was a capable editor and proof reader. She tackled the task with expertise and did so in a timely manner.

Bruce Moran is a publisher who not only delivers a first-class product but one who cares about his writers.

My dear family respects my need to not be disturbed when working and express interest in my progress.

I am truly blessed.

Printed in the USA
CPSIA information can be obtained
at www.ICGtesting.com
LVHW040600110923
757081LV00001B/28